Watercolor

By Leigh Talbert Moore

This book is a work of fiction. Names, characters, places, and incidents are products of the author's imagination or are used fictitiously. Any resemblance to actual events or locales or persons, living or dead, is entirely coincidental.

Watercolor
Copyright © Leigh Talbert Moore, 2013
www.leightmoore.com
Printed in the United States of America.

Cover design by Jolene B. Perry.

For my faithful readers and friends,
For everyone who believes in true love.
And for JRM, always~

Chapter 1

Two nights ago, I stood on the beach in Julian's arms watching as the New Year's Eve fireworks exploded in a brilliant finale. I kissed him, and we promised to spend the second half of senior year together.

Two hours before, I'd stood in a gigantic living room in a mansion on Hammond Island, the most exclusive neighborhood in our town, facing Julian's mystery father. I'd promised to keep him informed about Julian without ever revealing his identity.

Tonight, I stood in my bedroom, a cool January breeze blowing in across the Gulf, holding the one piece of evidence that could blow everything—a letter from Julian's mom to his dad, Bill Kyser.

I had to get that letter back to Julian's dad before anyone found it in my possession.

Winter had arrived in South County at last. My house was too far from the water to hear the waves crashing, but I'd opened my bedroom window and taken off the screen. Standing by my dresser, I closed my eyes and pretended I was out there, sitting on the shore, letting the damp, salty air push my hair around my face. In that moment, I could smell the crisp ocean water, and if I really focused, I could almost taste it.

Taste carried my mind back to Friday night, when I'd stood on the shore with Julian's arms tight around my waist. After two years we were officially together, and a little thrill followed closely by a smile hit me whenever I remembered that night.

He'd run down from his house to meet me at the public beach, and we'd stood on the shore watching the show. At midnight when we kissed, a hint of salt filled my mouth. I wasn't sure if it was from the running or the briny air or if everything about him was like the best day at the beach ever. It was probably all three.

In my quiet house, I remembered the other part of that night, and going to my door, I put my ear against it to listen. The only sound was silence. I turned the knob and carefully eased it open. No one was awake. Closing it again, I locked it and went to my dresser. In the top drawer, past panties, socks, and tights, I felt it. The letter. Right beside a little box.

I was dressed for bed in a tank top and snowman PJ pants. My curly brown hair was pulled into a side ponytail, and I hopped onto my bed holding both items from my drawer. The box contained the dragonfly ring Julian had made for me last semester. I slipped it onto my finger and dropped back on the bed on my back. Holding my hand up, I tilted it from side to side so the crystals would sparkle. It was possibly the best gift I'd ever received in my life, and thinking about officially being Julian's girlfriend filled my chest with a bubble of excitement.

Still smiling, I sat up again and grabbed the letter. It was the first time I'd read it since it fell out of Bill Kyser's private journal. That night, I'd stuffed it under my pillow, and later I'd forgotten to retrieve it before returning the secret books to Julian's dad. Now it was the only piece of evidence tying me to their story.

Carefully, I removed the thick paper from the light blue envelope and unfolded it.

Dear Bill,

Thank you again for the welding torch. I hope it will help Julian with his scholarship projects for SCAD. I'll be sure you know how that goes. His art is edgy and inventive, if a bit expensive. Perhaps he got a few developer genes from his father after all. Or maybe all boys like building things and playing with fire.

Speaking of fire, I also received your message about telling him about you. I understand you want to be in his life more, and I know it's been a long time. It's hard to believe thirteen years have passed since that terrible night.

But I still can't agree with you that telling Julian is the right thing. I think that would be playing with fire. And it would burn us badly. None of the children would recover from that wound.

For now, we must continue to keep your identity a secret. Julian has everything he needs, and you've always been so generous toward him. I thank you for that. Maybe one day he can know you as his father, but today, I just don't see how it's possible. I hope you understand.

Sincerely,
Alex

My fingers slid back and forth across the stationary. The letter was written after Julian's fifteenth birthday, three years ago. Apparently, Mr. Kyser had wanted to come clean. He'd wanted Julian to know the truth. That his father was the richest and possibly most powerful man in town.

My lips pressed together as my forehead creased. I'd promised I wouldn't tell Julian what I knew, but it was getting harder with every passing day.

Just then I heard a sharp *crack!* outside my window, followed by a snapping sound. Immediately, I dropped from my bed to the floor, eyes glued to the dark opening where my screen should've been. It was 12:30, and I had no idea what I'd do if a squirrel or something worse flew inside. In a blink, a dark head in a grey knit hat appeared. Shining blue eyes met mine, and my lips instantly broke into a smile to match the one on Julian's face.

"Anna?" he whispered, still outside. Then he strained to see me. "Are you hiding?"

My pulse raced. "What are you doing?" He couldn't see my hands, so I quickly folded the paper and shoved the incriminating letter back in its envelope as fast as I could.

"Coming to get you." He straddled my window sill, crossing over, and I slipped the letter under my bed before standing up.

Then I glanced down at what I was wearing—no bra, but my tank was black. "I was about to go to bed."

"Hmm," his eyes moved up and down my body, and I felt a little charge. "I miss warm weather."

"It'll be back soon."

His presence seemed to fill my room, as if he were the only thing there, dressed in dark jeans and a long-sleeved plaid shirt. I ran to him, and my bare feet made him seem even taller than usual. He pulled me by the waist into a close into a hug, and I shivered as his breath tickled past my ear.

"My vote's always for less clothes, but you're going to freeze." He straightened up, stepping over to my closet and digging around until he came back with my black hoodie. "Slip this on and some jeans."

I took it, not even thinking of putting up a fight. "What are we doing?"

"Meeting up with the guys down by the water," he whispered. "It's the last night before we head back to finish the year, and they wanted to hang out. I wanted to see you."

His words made me smile as I scooped a pair of faded jeans off the foot of my bed. He watched me a split second before going back to the window while I finished dressing. I grabbed my shoes and met him at the opening.

"Do you need help getting down?" He reached for the branch right outside.

"I don't know," I whispered, following him as I buttoned and zipped. "I've never done this before."

"That makes me very sad to hear. I'm definitely coming back."

My nose wrinkled, but I caught the hand he held out. Briefly, I slid my thumb across the tiny dragonfly tattoo he'd inked between his thumb and first finger. With our hands together, it looked like my ring and his ink were flying to each other.

"You're wearing it," he said. My eyes flickered to his, and just as fast, he leaned forward and kissed me, stealing my breath. His lips were warm against mine and sweet like fresh mint. "Mmm. I'd better get you down."

He caught my waist, helping me onto the branch. As always, I was surprised by his strength. Julian was tall and slim, but he was constantly lifting and holding up motorcycle parts and assorted machinery, the raw materials he welded into huge metal sculptures. It left him strong enough to take on guys twice his size, not that he needed to. His easy-going personality earned him friends just about every school circle.

9

Once across, I caught the branches and scrambled after him, quietly dashing across my front lawn and down the half-block to where his classic T-bird convertible was parked. We both jumped in, and I watched as he turned the key and waited.

For a second, the car only coughed and then went silent. My eyes blinked to his face, and I noticed his jaw clench.

"Second time this week," he muttered, giving the key another turn.

Still, it didn't start. He let out a low growl, and my shoulders tensed. "Piece of shit car," he swore.

"You love your car," I argued, hoping to be encouraging.

My excited mood faltered as he turned it once more, but the car roared to life. I quietly exhaled the breath I didn't realize I was holding.

"There," his brow relaxed, and he shot me a smile. "Good thing. I've got zero cash for car shopping."

"I'll pick you up if you ever need a ride to school or anything." I took his hand. He gave me a little pull, and I scooted across the bench seat, pressing my body into his side.

"Thanks, but I was hoping to be driving you to school. And we've got that art opening in Darplane next week. You still my date?"

"Wouldn't miss it." I rested my head on his shoulder. "I'm just saying, I'll help you whenever."

"My angel." He pressed his lips against my head. "But I've got things I want to do for you now."

I studied his profile. "You don't have to do anything for me."

His eyes were on the road. "I want to. After the opening, more stuff should start selling in Newhope. You just wait."

I shook my head, watching the road. I didn't want him to spend the little money he earned on me, but it was no use telling Julian what to do.

Down by the water, Brad Brennan was waiting with his girlfriend Rachel. He had built a small fire on the beach, and he was sitting on a huge driftwood log with her right in front of him. Brad was the quarterback for our high school football team, and Rachel was head cheerleader. They were the perfect cliché, but Fairview was a small town. They had been together since middle school, and while I never thought I'd be close friends with someone like Rachel, this year had changed everything. We were even planning to be roommates next fall if I got into college in New Orleans.

Julian and Brad had been inseparable since their near-fatal car crash fall semester, and knowing the history of their dads, I couldn't help wondering if some humans were destined to be friends.

Julian held my hand as we walked to join them, and Rachel's eyebrows rose at the sight of us together. I smiled, feeling my cheeks warm. It was our first public appearance as a couple.

"Hey, what's this about?" Brad teased us, nodding my way as he bumped fists with Julian.

"Yeah, we're together," Julian said, sitting and pulling me onto his lap.

A huge black guy sat nearby on the other side of the fire. He looked vaguely familiar to me, and I tried to remember if he was on the football team with Brad.

"Cool," Brad said as we sat. "You know Montage?"

Julian waved toward the guy. "Hey — Tamara's little bro?"

Montage nodded back, and instantly I recognized him. "Hey! Tamara does my hair," I said.

He nodded, and I wondered why he was here. Tamara had mentioned her little brother, but he lived in Crystal Shores, the next town over.

"Mo's transferring to Fairview to finish out the school year," Brad said.

"Kind of late to switch schools." Julian's arm went around my waist. My back was pressed against his chest, and it felt warm and right.

Montage studied the fire, his expression serious. "Stupid shit's going down at Crystal Shores. I'm moving in with Tamara."

Brad glanced at him. "You don't have to worry about anything happening at Fairview. Coach Wilson keeps a close eye on things, and his uncle's a cop. First cousin's the mayor."

"The school's just so spread out," our new friend said.

My brow creased. I didn't understand what they were talking about or why Montage would be worrying about the layout of our campus, but I didn't like it. His switching schools at the very end of senior year meant it was probably something serious.

"What's going on?" I asked. Julian's arm squeezed my waist.

Montage shrugged. "A guy at Crystal Shores says I intentionally hurt him last season in a game. Killed his chance at a scholarship. Now he wants revenge."

"He made some serious threats," Brad added. "But it's all bullshit. This time next year, it'll be ancient history."

Julian's chin was on my shoulder, so his voice was close to my ear, as if he were speaking just to comfort me. "If the principal and the coaches know, they'll be watching out for you."

"Wait—you think some guy might try and hurt you at Fairview?" Rachel studied Brad and Montage's faces, her brow creased as well.

"I'd like to see him try." Brad's voice reminded me of his dad's, all tough swagger and arrogance. It did little to ease my growing concern. "Football's a tough game. Deal with it."

Montage shook his head and looked forward. "I'm just hoping it stays back there."

Julian jumped in, giving me a quick squeeze before standing. "I say we don't borrow trouble. If something happens, we'll handle it, and it's more likely nothing will."

Brad made a noise of agreement and pulled out a flask from his coat pocket. "Here's to the last days ahead." He took a shot and motioned to Rachel. She waved it away, and he tossed the thin silver container to Julian.

He grinned and took a quick hit. I pressed my lips together, but he kissed me fast before tossing it to Montage. Montage just held it a moment and then shook his head. "I don't need any more trouble."

Brad took the flask back and slapped him on the shoulder. "We've got you covered, my man."

He took another drink and with that, the guys were talking about senior bowl and who'd be in Sterling in a few months representing the college teams. Brad had surprised everyone by opting to go to Tulane in New Orleans instead of one of the big state schools that had been after him. I thought about the journals and what I'd read about his dad. The Brennans could be unpredictable fellows. Montage was headed to State, and judging by his size, I figured he'd been recruited just as hard as Brad.

Rachel's brow was still lined, and she listened to them talking in silence. I could tell she was as troubled by what the guys said as I was, but they were too busy swapping drinks and talking football to notice. Before long, Julian was back sitting beside me. Rachel was talking about the events remaining for the year. In addition to head cheerleader, she was chair of the party planning committee and senior liaison for prom. They were working on a spring dance, a bonfire to kick off spring break, of course prom... It sounded like she'd be working nonstop as she listed all the social activities they had planned before graduation.

"We're hoping the bonfire will be the start of a class tradition," she said, and I didn't even realize I was falling asleep until my head dropped forward on Julian's shoulder.

"Hey," he caught my chin, and I felt my cheeks flush. He laughed. "Rachel, you're putting everybody to sleep. We're taking off."

"No, she's not," I said, shaking my head, but Julian pulled me up. I waved, and we all said goodnight. This time the car cranked without hesitation, and before long we were back at my house standing outside Julian's car.

"The one bad thing about sneaking out is getting back in," he said, staring up at the tree.

My eyes traveled to my window. I was way too tired for climbing. "I'll get the hidden key and use the door."

"Where's the fun in that?" Julian teased, catching me around the waist and pulling me to him. My hands went to his shoulders. "See you tomorrow?"

I nodded, threading my fingers into the soft hair just brushing the top of his collar.

He leaned down. "Thanks for coming out." Warm lips met mine, pushing them apart and sending a wave of sparkling happiness straight to my stomach. His tongue curled to mine, and the chills made a little noise come from my throat.

"Mmm," he breathed, resting his forehead on mine. "You use the door, I'll meet you upstairs."

My eyes were closed, and electricity hummed just under my skin. "We can't stay awake all night," I whispered.

"I could." He lifted his head and kissed my nose, eyes shining. "But you're right. School tomorrow."

I nodded, slowly backing toward my house. Our arms stretched out, fingers laced until we were too far apart to hold on anymore, I smiled and dashed to the door, giving him one last look before reaching into the ivy for the hidden key.

Chapter 2

Rachel was the first person I saw at school the next day. "So you and Julian," she said, eyebrows up. "And where does that put Jack Kyser in the rankings now?"

My pace skipped a beat as I followed her into the building. "You know we broke up," I said, not wanting to think about my days last fall with Mr. Kyser's well-known son.

Her head rocked side to side. "And then you got back together and then you broke up and then—"

"All right, but now it's definitely over."

She grinned, pushing a lock of straight blonde hair behind her shoulder. "If you say so, but you were *way* into him. I remember."

"First, you're being super uncool, and second, you know how long I've liked Julian."

She nodded. "You think you can keep up with Julian?"

"What do you mean?" Privately, I had already been thinking the same thing.

We stopped at her locker. "Renee and I are friends, so I know how he is. He's not one to say no. To anything. And you're, well..."

"A nun?"

She made a teasing face. "I was going to say 'new at all this.'"

I shook my head. "Says the girl who's dated the same guy since middle school."

"Brad and I mesh well," she winked. "Very well."

"Okay!" I breathed, leaning back against the locker beside hers.

Now all I could think of was Renee, Julian's former hook-up buddy. "What's the opposite of a nun?"

Rachel laughed, but I was serious. "Actually, things between us are great. We're taking it slow. And, well, I'm not planning to tell Julian no."

My friend's eyebrows rose as she slammed her locker door. "Okay, then. I guess that's settled."

I shrugged, walking with her the short distance to my locker. "I'm just taking it as it comes."

"Are you going with him to Darplane?"

I nodded. "Of course."

We were at my locker now, and I spotted Julian headed our way with Brad. "Ready for the final round?" he said, leaning beside me.

"Hey, Julian," Rachel said then she elbowed me. "Here's to a memorable spring."

She twirled off with Brad, and Julian nodded, watching them go. "Too bad spring means no more uniforms." Then his eyes landed on mine, shooting that warmth straight to my core. "So how come you never joined the squad? You'd look great in one of those skirts."

I pressed my lips into a frown. "Renee Barron sure held your attention in hers."

"Hey," he caught my waist. "Why are you bringing her up?"

"Rachel did," I shook my head, looking down. "I don't know why I said that. I'm sorry."

"Accepted." He kissed the side of my neck, and I almost squealed.

"But I'm not sorry she graduated early and moved on," I added.

"To Fulton community college," he teased. "That's just right up the road."

My eyes narrowed. "You planning to look her up?"

He laughed. "That's nuts. Ridiculous. But I like how green your eyes are today."

"Shut up."

The truth was, Renee did bother me — not because I was afraid Julian was still into her, but because of what I imagined he was used to getting from her. I was majorly inexperienced compared to Renee, and even though Julian hadn't attempted anything yet, I was nervous about embarrassing myself with my naiveté.

Montage stopped to speak, and his story from last night flashed through my mind. They joked around, and I wondered how serious those threats the massive linebacker had mentioned were. Julian might be strong enough to lift me, but he was no match for guys like Montage.

Turning to my locker, I wondered what Julian's dad would say if I told him about it. Could he help without the truth coming out? And if the truth did come out, would Julian be super-pissed at me? The swirl of problems in my head was triggering a migraine when…

Julian touched my cheek. "Anna?"

My worried eyes snapped to his. "Yeah?"

"Why are you looking like you found a severed head in your locker?"

I forced a laugh, not about to tell him where my mind was. "I'm not! I'm just…" searching for anything, "What's the deal with us going to Darplane? What day and when?"

"Tuesday. The letter said it starts at 6:30, so I guess we should leave by 5:30 to get there on time. Are you thinking your parents won't let you go?"

"I'm almost positive Mom will push me out the door."

The bell rang, and he gave me a quick kiss. "Great," he said, catching my waist. "And don't worry about that deal with Mo."

My eyes flickered down. "It's kind of hard not to."

He caught my chin, forcing me to meet his blue eyes. "Those guys wouldn't be dumb enough to try something at our school. If anything did happen, it would be out somewhere."

"That's not very encouraging."

He leaned in and kissed me again, softer. "Chances are better nothing's going to happen."

I took a deep breath and nodded. Then he took off as I headed into English class. If Julian was right, there wasn't much point worrying. I looked around the room—all the same faces with one notable exception. English was the class Jack and I had shared last semester, and the one topic that had brought us together. Sitting at my desk, my eyes flickered to the door, and clear as a bell in my memory, I could see him standing there, blue eyes shining, messy blonde hair, perfectly handsome face. He called me a sexy librarian. My throat tightened, but I clenched my jaw. I was *not* doing this. Jack was gone, and even if he wasn't, I didn't care. I was with Julian now.

Glancing to his old seat, I caught the eye of a large-nosed female classmate now sitting there. She smiled awkwardly, and I smiled back before blinking down. The absurdity of it all made me laugh. The tension in my shoulders loosened, and I straightened up, looking around the class. Summer Daigle watched me from the back corner, so I waved. She smiled. Mrs. Bowman walked in and began speaking, and I dragged out my composition book.

After first period, I waited for Summer as my fellow classmates all pushed into the hall.

"Oh, hey, Anna," she said. Summer always sounded like she was in a daze.

"Hi!" I said, turning to walk with her. "How's your year going? We didn't see each other much first semester."

"Yeah. You're like a different person now." She studied the floor ahead of us. "Are you still dating Jack Kyser?"

I kept my voice light. "No, he graduated and moved to New Orleans. He's at Tulane now."

"You used to look at him like he was a god."

How embarrassing! "Umm... I did? I guess I really liked him."

"That must've been why he was so into you," she stopped at her locker and started dialing. "It was like you worshipped him or something."

My jaw dropped. "I'd like to think he dated me for more than that," I recovered. "And I don't know that I *worshipped* him."

"If you say so." She stared into the open space.

I'd had enough of this misstep. "Well, later, Summer. I'll tell Gabi we have class together," I turned to leave, but she caught me.

"You still talk to Gabi?" Her forehead was lined. "I figured you were too cool for her now."

Everything in my head was screaming to disengage. "Why would you think that?"

"Because you're hanging out with Rachel and Brad. I don't think you talked to me once last fall."

I was starting to see why. "I guess I was a little distracted. But I'm talking to you now! See you in class tomorrow?"

She shrugged. "Whatever."

I nodded and took off, realizing I was completely wrong about Summer. She wasn't quirky, she was just plain weird. And rude. Nobody said stuff like that to another person. She was practically insulting me. What was wrong with her? Me worshipping Jack. Me too cool for Gabi...

"You're ticked." It was Julian. "And where's the fire? Slow down."

"I just attempted to have a conversation with Summer Daigle."

He laughed out loud. "Talk about speaking your mind. That girl is crazy."

"I know! What's wrong with her?" I was at my locker, dialing angrily. "Is she on drugs or something?"

"Don't think so." Julian slung his arm across my shoulders. "What did she say? Something about your hair?"

My eyes flew wide. "What's wrong with my hair?" Quickly I snatched the band off my wrist to tie back my light brown curls. "Is it big?"

"Your hair looks great. Stop it." Julian took the band away. "I was just trying to guess how she could've pissed you off."

I exhaled and dropped my hands. "She said something about me being too cool to talk to Gabi..."

"You still talk to Gabi?" His forehead creased.

"Julian!" I shoved his shoulder, and he laughed again.

"No, I'm really surprised." He caught my hand, still grinning. "Not because you're cool or anything."

"Thanks."

"Seriously. I think it's nice you guys keep up. I liked Gabi."

The feeling was very mutual, I thought. "I need to call her, actually," I said.

"Hey, so Ms. Clayton busted me coasting through Algebra II," he said, still holding my hand. "Gave me the final for the mid-term and I aced it. Now I'm in advanced math."

"With me?" I couldn't stop the big smile on my face, but just as fast, I frowned. "You can't flunk it."

"I'll try," he reached up and tugged a curl. "But you know how distracting you can be."

We arrived at class just as Mrs. Harris stepped out the door. "Party's over. Break it up and find your seats."

For the first half of the class, I kept fighting the urge to glance at him. It was our first class together as a couple, and now when I looked at him, he looked... yummy. The next time I glanced back, he caught my eye and made a face. I nearly laughed, and Mrs. Harris asked me to repeat what she'd said. I had no idea. When I glanced again, Julian's eyes were very disapproving. I giggled and started taking notes. Everything felt brighter now, and I was convinced final semester was going to rock.

Chapter 3

Mom was digging in a kitchen cabinet with half her body inside the lower shelf when I got home. I dropped my books on the table and went over to her.

"What are you doing" I asked.

She screamed and banged her head. "Anna! You do *not* sneak up on people like that."

My eyebrows flew up. "I threw my books on the table as loud as I possibly could! What are you hiding?"

"I'm not hiding anything." She crawled out, groaning and rubbing her back. "I'm trying to find my lasagna pan."

I grabbed a box of crackers out of the cabinet. "Dad threw it out. Said it was making him fat or something."

"Your dad is vain," she complained, dusting her hands. "And I want lasagna."

"You kids'll have to work this one out yourselves," I teased. Mom rolled her eyes and went back to digging.

"So Julian's having this big reception in Darplane next Tuesday," I started, "and he asked if I'd go with him."

"The one at the Athletic Center? That's going to be such a big deal for him. *And* it's outside South County, which is huge. Wish I could go."

My brows pulled together. "Why can't you go?"

At that she stood up, sighing. "I'm changing out the featured artist's work at the association. I said I'd do it, and now I'm stuck. Everyone's going to Darplane."

"Well, Julian will be very disappointed." I hopped up on the counter. "I think he likes you better than me."

She laughed and shook her head. "Julian's a flirt. You keep your eyes on him."

"With pleasure!" I smiled, crunching a cracker. "So can I go?"

"Of course!" she grabbed a cracker and leaned against the bar. "You'll have to dress up. And you'll probably be out late." I nodded, and she continued. "But it's cultural education. And he should be able to get you home by eleven."

"Okay!" I jumped down excited. "I'll let him know."

"Hang on, young lady. One thing," she gave me a stern look. "They have champagne at those events, and you do *not* have permission to drink it."

"Oh," I exhaled, my shoulders dropping. "Mom. I'm sure they'll have people watching us, and we're obviously underage."

"Still," she continued. "Adults at these things might be irresponsible. They think because it's Julian's big night, it's okay for him to have champagne, and it's not. You guys have a long drive back."

I chewed my lip, thinking about Julian and Brad's flask swapping. "I never drink, Mom." Silently adding *now*. The night of the car crash, when Julian almost died had totally cured me.

"Good." She patted my shoulder. "And if Julian does, you drive."

That I could answer with confidence. "Deal."

"A-ha!" She pulled out a long, rectangular pan and set it on the counter.

I grinned. "I'm going upstairs. Call me when the evil lasagna's ready."

"Oh, it won't be til tomorrow." She went to the sink and turned on the faucet. "I've got to soak the noodles and get everything ready. I just wanted to be sure I had the pan. We're ordering pizza tonight."

"Mom!" I rolled my eyes and ran upstairs as my phone rang. It was my boss from the paper, Nancy Riggs. "Nancy, Hi!"

"Hey, Anna!" I could hear her smiling. "You coming back this semester?"

"Of course!" I flopped on my bed. "I was going to drop by this week and see if you still wanted me or if you were planning to find someone else."

"No way! You were the best student intern we've had in a while. I'd never have gotten those archives on the computer if you hadn't done all that extra work."

Nancy had no clue I'd discovered the secret of Julian's parents, and working in the archives was a big part of confirming what I'd suspected. "It just made sense," I said. "We were doing that insert, and it made finding things so much easier."

"And," she continued. "You were able to get Alex LaSalle to agree to that interview. Normally, it takes years to develop the skills to bag a reluctant subject. You even had Bill Kyser ready to work with you."

Chewing my lip, I didn't answer. Nancy also didn't know they'd agreed to the interviews in an effort to silence what I knew about Julian. Even though I hadn't threatened them. I'd only told them I wished *they* would tell Julian the truth, which had led his mom into full panic-mode. I shook my head.

"You know Curtis has connections at the *Times-Picayune*. The New Orleans paper?" I could hear her pencil tapping on her desk. "He could probably help you get a student job while you're at Loyola next year. He might even be able to get you some scholarship money. You're majoring in journalism, right?"

"Oh my god, yes!" I cried. "But I haven't been accepted yet."

I'd applied to all the New Orleans schools last fall when I'd discovered Jack was going to Tulane. A few weeks later, we had broken up, but my applications were already in the mail.

"Oh, you will be," Nancy said with confidence. "I'll make a note to talk to him about it. So when can you start?"

"When do you need me?"

"School just started back?" Her voice grew thoughtful. "How 'bout you get in your groove and check in once you're ready. Say a few weeks?"

"Sure! Hey, I'm going with Julian LaSalle to that reception at the Athletic Center. Maybe I could start then?"

"I need someone to take pictures there," she said. "I'll pay you if we're able to print them. And you'll get a photo credit, so do a good job."

My chest was bursting with excitement. "Done! And I'll stick my head in this week."

"No pressure," Nancy said with a laugh. "And same deal, right? Five hours a week?"

"Or more, I guess."

We hung up, and I almost squealed. If I got a decent picture in the paper, that was another clip for my portfolio. *Thank you, Julian!* I flopped on my bed and pulled out my books.

School was buzzing with Julian's big event by Thursday, and even the morning announcements gave him a little shout out. "So your mom's cool with you being out late tonight, right?" he asked as we made our way to calculus.

I nodded. "Of course! She said something about how we shouldn't have any trouble being home by eleven."

His lips pressed into a frown. "There goes the fake breakdown."

"Julian!" I laughed. He grinned, catching my hand and pulling it to his lips. My insides warmed and my bottom lip caught in my teeth. I loved when he kissed me.

"I'll pick you up," he said. "And I'm the star so dress hot."

I pulled up close to him, his lips still hovering over my fingers. "I think I know how to dress for an art reception."

He grinned. "I'm sure you do."

Ms. Harris appeared, and we dropped hands, stepping into class. Our math teacher didn't tolerate celebrities, but it didn't matter. The reception was going to be amazing.

Chapter 4

Julian's knock was right on time. Dad was out of town, and Mom had stayed at the association to work on the art display. I pulled up my long black skirt and carefully jogged down the stairs in my heels, but when I opened the door, I froze. Julian was dressed in jeans and a white tee, a black leather jacket and chucks.

"What are you wearing?" I said.

He shrugged. "I'm the artist. I went for quirky."

"You look like a rocker."

He nodded, looking down. "That's cool. A lot of artists start bands."

My lips pressed together as I evaluated my conservative outfit. I looked like I was headed to the opera. "I've got to change."

"Not the top. I like sequins."

"Hang on," I ran up the stairs. "I'll just slip on some dark jeans. You know, I think these guys are all ex-Marines. They're not going to be impressed."

Julian followed me into my room and flopped across my bed. "How about a quickie to get us in the mood?"

I froze mid-change, thinking of what I'd told Rachel. I wasn't planning to tell him no, but I wasn't prepared for my yes to happen now. "A quickie? But..." He started to laugh, and I realized he was teasing. "Julian! Get out of here."

He rolled onto his back. "I'll close my eyes."

"I'm going to the bathroom." I grabbed my jeans and ran across the hall. "Where's your mom?" I shouted. "I thought for sure she'd be at this."

"She's meeting us there," he yelled back. "I think she has a boyfriend now."

"What?" Jumping to open the door, I slammed my head against the cabinet. I was still fastening my pants when I ran back into my room. "Your mom has a boyfriend?"

The corner of his mouth rose as he watched me return half-dressed. "Changed your mind?"

I glanced down, continuing to fasten my jeans. "You just said your mom has a boyfriend? Who?"

"Whoa, slow down." He sat up. "I don't know anything for sure, but she's been getting mysterious calls that make her blush and act... *not* like my mom."

I chewed my lip. "That's pretty thin. It could be a million other things."

He bounced forward on the bed, catching my waist and pulling me to him. "And I saw her slip out one night after she thought I was asleep." He lifted my sequined top and kissed my bare stomach. Electricity flashed to my toes.

"Julian," I gasped, catching his cheeks.

"I think it's a boyfriend," he said, kissing me again.

My knees had turned to Jell-O, and a tingly sensation had settled low in my stomach. "We'll be late," I managed to say.

He sighed, sliding off the bed. While I tried to refocus my brain, I couldn't help wondering if it were possible... were Julian's parents hooking up? I studied his face, thinking. "Would you mind?"

"What? If Mom had a guy?" He shrugged. "I guess not. I mean, if he's nice to her and all. What difference does it make to me? I'm leaving in a year."

—
32

I nodded. "How's this?" I was now wearing dark jeans with my short-sleeved sequined top and black ballet flats.

"Perfect."

But I wasn't done. I stepped over to my dresser and pulled out the small box. I flipped the top off and unwrapped the tissue I kept it in, putting the sparkling dragonfly ring on my finger. "Now it's perfect."

He stood and held my finger, turning it to make the light reflect off the crystals. I watched the corners of his blue eyes crease as he smiled.

"What are you thinking?" I said.

"Huh?"

"You look like you know something I don't. Is there a bug in it now?" I teased, sliding the ring around on my finger. "Or a tiny camera?"

"That would be awesome," he laughed. "A bugged bug. Why didn't I think of that?"

"Seriously." I said, holding his hand, my thumb sliding back and forth over his little matching dragonfly tat.

"I don't know," he shrugged. "It just feels right, I guess. I'm trying to be cool here, okay?"

"Okay." I said because it did feel right.

He bent down to kiss me, and I slid my arms around his neck. The familiar rush of excitement flooded my body, and images of us at the hay maze last fall in Springdale filled my thoughts, our mouths moving faster, hands everywhere.

"We probably have a few extra minutes," he said sitting down on the bed.

"We do not!" I laughed, pulling him back up. "You're going to be late, and you're the star. Let's go."

"Rockers are always late," he said, leaning down again.

I ducked and ran out of the room and down the stairs, grabbing my purse off the bar.

We arrived in Darplane with plenty of time to spare before the reception. As we drove in, I noticed the blooming crepe myrtles planted down the median of the highway. They were beautiful, and the fading light of the setting sun cast everything in a pinkish hue.

"Hey, let me show you something," Julian said, turning the car north toward Fort Spain.

"Where are we going?" I checked the time.

"Hang on. I want you to see this."

He drove the car over the Interstate and up a steep hill into the small town. Fort Spain was high on the bluffs of Sterling Bay. At the top, Julian made a U-turn and started driving back down the same way toward Darplane.

I looked around, over my shoulder. "Did I miss it? What are we doing?"

As we made our way back toward the Interstate, Julian dropped his speed. "Look at the bay," he said.

The sun was hidden behind long, thin clouds that were glowing neon pink, and the sky was alternating shades of blue, purple, pink, orange, and yellow. The water was a shimmering electric rose, and dotted throughout, all the way to the horizon, were little white sailboats. Occasionally a brown pelican or a group of seagulls would swoop down.

My breath caught. "Oh, Julian!" I whispered. "It's so beautiful. Is it always like this?"

He smiled, touching my shoulder. "Only when the sun sets that way. I thought about it when we were driving in, and I wanted to see how it looked. Mom could capture that perfectly on canvas."

I couldn't tear my eyes away. "Has she ever painted the bay?"

His eyes were back on the road. "I don't know, but it's her style."

I took a picture with the camera I'd thrown in my bag, and I remembered my other job for the night. "Hey, Nancy asked if I would get some shots of you for the paper, so be cooperative, okay?"

His brow creased. "You're not working on our date, are you?"

I slid across the bench seat and kissed his cheek. "Just a tiny bit," I said. "And it's going to give me clips, so this is a big deal for me, too."

We were at the center, and his lips tightened. "I think we're going to have to walk." The parking lot was completely filled, and cars were even lining the road. "You'd think they'd save me a spot."

I squeezed his arm. "You build to that, I guess."

We parked on the side of a hill near a little strip mall hidden in the trees and slowly picked out a walking path to our destination. It was also hidden in the trees, I wondered if most people driving by even realized it was here. My thoughts were distracted when I realized Julian had stopped.

"Hey," I went back, catching his arm. "What's wrong? You're not nervous are you?"

He stood straight, looking up at the huge building. "What do you think they'll expect me to do?"

"Feats of welding, I'm sure. Did you pack your blowtorch?"

He blinked to me. "No."

"I was only joking," I snorted, looping my arm through his and pulling him to the door. "I'm sure you'll just stand around being charming. Easy!" Then I poked his side gently. "Into the lion's den?" It was the same thing he'd said the night we drove together to Jack and Lucy's birthday party.

He leaned over and kissed my cheek. "I'm glad you're with me."

"Me, too."

Inside the massive, open lobby, photographs of Julian's pieces were on easels and tables filled with hors d'oeuvres, cheese platters, and small desserts were arranged around them. Male and female waiters circled the room carrying trays of hot appetizers and champagne flutes. We wound our way through the crowd, and I saw Lucy Kyser standing beside one of the easels. She wore a light blue silk dress, and her blonde hair streamed down her back in shimmering waves. As always, she looked like a model, and I couldn't help thinking of what I'd read about her mother. I imagined they looked just alike.

"I'll grab us something to drink," Julian said, squeezing my hand. I nodded, and as he left, I went over to her.

"Anna!" Lucy shrieked when she saw me, grabbing me in a hug. "I didn't know you'd be here. You look fantastic!"

"I was just about to say the same to you!" I hugged my friend, and when she smiled, I felt a twinge. Twins, she and Jack had the exact same clear blue eyes. Just like their dad's—and her secret half-brother's.

"What are you doing here?" I asked, hooking our arms.

"Oh, I rode over with Dad," she said as we walked through the display. "B.J.'s coming to drive me home."

My brows pulled together. "Why all the musical cars?"

She shrugged. "Dad has to meet someone after, but B.J.'s working on a project with Sterling Bay Watch. So I asked if I could tag along. Can you believe how amazing this stuff is? Julian's so great."

"I know," I smiled trying not to look smug. I reminded myself that it was only a matter of time before Julian would've been discovered. My first news feature on his art didn't really give me bragging rights.

"So I talked to Jack last night," she said, pulling my arm. "He's not dating anyone. You know what that means..."

I was stunned by her words and could only shake my head as she continued.

"He is *so* waiting for you," she giggled. "I'm going down there next weekend. Want to tag along and drop in?"

"No!" I almost shouted, then I cleared my throat. "I told you at Christmas. We broke up —"

"And it was completely ridiculous!" she cried. "You could so easily be together still and save all this pointless moping. Seriously. Two months and not a single date? He just goes out with Will or alone. It's pitiful."

Her words gave me heartburn. Why would Jack be moping? He'd broken up with me! Lucy liked exaggeration, so I decided to believe this was more of the same. Jack could very well be dating someone and she just didn't know. After all, she didn't know he and I had broken up. Just then Julian returned.

He paused for a beat in front of Lucy, and I couldn't breathe seeing the two of them together, knowing their connection. They actually looked more alike to me now—more like the siblings they didn't know they were.

"Julian. Hi," Lucy said, looking down.

"Hi, Lucy." He leaned forward and gave her a quick hug. "It's been a while."

"Right." Her cheeks flushed. "Not since the accident—"

"You know what?" he interrupted. "Let's just forget about that. It's all good, right?"

He smiled, and I wanted to kiss him again. Instead, I put my hand in the crook of his arm and gave him a squeeze. He stepped aside to grab an appetizer and Lucy quickly leaned in to me.

"Are you two dating now?" Her eyes narrowed.

"Oh… uhh…" I panicked imagining her telling Jack. Then I shook myself. Who cared if she told Jack? "Yes! We kind of just started over the break."

"That explains why you don't want to go to New Orleans with me," she said louder.

Julian was back, and I felt him glance at me. Then Lucy saw the ring on my finger.

"Oh! It's just like mine," she said. "Let me see it!"

Julian's first attempt at jewelry-making was a delicate band composed of a series of tiny silver shells. It had been a birthday present for Lucy, and when I'd said I loved it, he'd made mine.

"I should've worn it," she continued. "I completely forgot, and it would be the perfect thing."

"Did I miss the party?" A tall, dark, and super-friendly fellow walked up and slid his hand around Lucy's waist, kissing her cheek.

"B.J.," she hugged her boyfriend. "This is our star, Julian LaSalle, and my dear friend Anna Sanders."

He shook Julian's hand, but studied me. "Have we met before?"

"Not really," I said, thinking of that day last summer. "I mean, I talked to you at the beach one day when you were life guarding."

Just then one of the officials came up to our group. "Julian LaSalle?" the man asked.

"Present," Julian said.

The man assessed our casual attire with a small frown. "We need you over here to work out the unveiling."

"I'll be back." Julian squeezed my arm before disappearing.

Lucy sidled up to me. "I guess Jack might be waiting, but you're not."

"We didn't say we'd wait," I said feeling guilty, which was stupid.

She smiled at me. "Look, you don't have to sell Julian on me. I know."

I wondered what she'd say if she also knew he was her half-brother. "Lucy, please don't say anything to Jack."

"Like what?" she played innocent. I watched her stroll away with B.J. leaving me with the question. I didn't know what I didn't want her to tell Jack. I didn't know why I cared. She could tell him whatever she wanted. I hoped she *did* tell him Julian and I were together. Then maybe the stupid pain that tried to creep into my chest at her saying he was alone and waiting for me would be gone for good.

"Anna?" A familiar voice snapped me to attention.

"Oh!" I jumped. "Mr. Kyser!"

He looked around, brows drawn together. "I told you I'd be here."

"Right," I nodded, remembering our conversation at his house the night I returned the three journals. "You came for Julian."

"I need to speak to you," he said in a lower voice. "Did you bring the *other* item?"

I knew at once he meant the letter. "I'm sorry," I said, looking down. "There wasn't a way…"

"Dad?" Lucy was back. "B.J.'s here, so you're free of me."

His expression was still stern, but he kissed his only daughter's temple. "I'm staying a little longer." He seemed to be avoiding looking at her. "There are some people here I want to speak to."

"Well, thanks for the ride," she said in a small voice. Watching them was heartbreaking. I wanted to believe things were improving between them, but I couldn't tell.

Mr. Kyser turned to go, but he paused. "Are you still working for the paper?"

"Yes, sir," I nodded.

"Good," was all he said before leaving me and going to the bar.

I shook my head and wandered off to find Julian. He was with his mother looking at one of the photographs of his work. Ms. LaSalle wore a long, red dress, and her dark brown hair hung loosely down her back. Her dark eyes glowed, and everything about her was relaxed and happy. She smiled at her only child as if he had just risen to national prominence.

"I've got a few more minutes," he told me, slipping his arm around my waist.

"Hi, Ms. LaSalle," I said.

"Anna, I've told you to call me Alex."

I shook my head. "I know, but it's too weird."

Julian nodded then gave me a squeeze. "That guy's signaling me to go out front for the whole unveiling thing. You want to hang with Mom?" I agreed, and he pulled my hair back, kissing my neck loudly before walking away.

I glanced back at his mom, my cheeks hot. "He's so crazy," I said with a little laugh.

She just shook her head, but once he was gone, her expression grew more serious. "Thank you, Anna," she said in a lower tone. "I'm sure it's difficult being with him, knowing what you know. But I appreciate your silence."

"I promised you I wouldn't tell him. But I wish you would."

A server passed by, and she lifted a champagne flute from his tray. "He would only be hurt by the truth," she said, taking a sip.

Just then the school's director called for our attention. We all went outside to the front lawn where a large white sheet was draped over a huge figure. It was a beautiful night, still warm but with a slight breeze. The director was making a speech about the importance of supporting local art and the spirit of youth, about Julian's talent and his embodiment of the spirit of local youth. My eyes wandered through the crowd as he spoke.

Mr. Kyser stood near the back holding a drink and talking to another man who looked about his age. Lucy stood with B.J., who had his arm across her shoulders. My eyes rose to the side of the center, which was covered in several large murals of athletes engaged in different sporting events, and I was distracted when everyone began clapping and the veil over Julian's runner dropped. I quickly pulled out my camera and took a shot of him shaking hands with Dr. Konrad.

The runner was one of Julian's most imaginative pieces. It had a motorcycle wheel for a head, complete with fender, which served as a helmet. The quads were bicycle chains with sprockets for knees. Exhaust-pipes formed the arms and levers made up the lower legs. The hands were shaped from copper tubing and the entire statue leaned forward at an angle. It looked as if it were frozen pushing off from the starting peg, and you could almost hear the pistol firing. It was enormous, and I tried to imagine how much work it had been for him welding it together. Using the torch his father had sent for his birthday.

The clapping subsided, and Julian hopped off the platform, making his way to where we were standing. A dull roar grew from low voices all speaking at once, and the crowd started moving again.

"So there you go," he said, tossing an arm across my shoulders. "Young America, local art, and all that."

"You're definitely in the club now." I laced my fingers in his.

Mr. Kyser walked over to us with the man I'd noticed him talking to during the speech. "Congratulations, Julian," he said in a serious tone.

Julian straightened up, lowering his arm.

"I wanted to introduce you to an old friend of mine," Mr. Kyser continued, "Chris Irvine of Studio 909 in Sterling. I was telling him you might have some pieces for his gallery."

"Hi, nice to meet you," Julian said quickly, stepping forward to shake hands. "Thanks for coming out."

Mr. Kyser stepped over and put his hand on Julian's shoulder. "Chris this is my… ah…"

My eyes widened, and I almost choked when he hesitated. *Was he about to introduce Julian as his son?* Ms. LaSalle appeared, pulling me away from the group.

"Anna, are you okay?" she said, her voice stern.

I nodded, and Julian hadn't noticed.

"My friend?" Mr. Kyser continued as if nothing had happened. "Would that be correct to say, Julian?"

"Yes, sir," Julian answered. "I mean, sure."

"This is great stuff," Mr. Irvine said. "Here's my card. You call me when you have some pieces ready for me. Bill's always been a good client. I'd be glad to carry your work."

"I'm sorry," I whispered to Ms. LaSalle, but her expression was annoyed. I was completely flustered. "Do you mind if I take your picture? It's for the Fairview paper."

"Sure!" Julian stood between his mom and Mr. Kyser with Mr. Irvine over to the right. I couldn't wait to make a print of this one.

The rest of the night was more of the same. Julian was introduced to gallery owners and civic leaders, and I stood by smiling and snapping pictures of him and them and his work. After another hour, I looked around and Mr. Kyser was gone. I didn't see Lucy anywhere, and I couldn't even spot Ms. LaSalle in the crowd.

Finally, Julian was back by my side. "You ready to get out of here? I'm dead."

"You sure?" My forehead wrinkled. "I don't want you to miss anyone."

"I stopped remembering names an hour ago," he said under his breath.

I giggled as we slipped out of a side exit in the back.

"I think we stayed long enough to get you launched," I said as we jogged to his car.

The parking lot was emptying.

"I guess. I don't know." He looked back at the huge structure. "At least Earl looks cool out front."

"Earl?" My nose wrinkled. "Is that what we're calling him?"

Julian shrugged. We were at his car, and he leaned back against it. "I got bored during that speech, and I decided he deserved a name. I was torn between Raphael and Earl."

I leaned beside him, and we studied the far-off center with its new lawn ornament. "I think he's more a Raphael myself with that motorcycle head."

"Yeah, but this is south Alabama." Julian pushed away from the car, opening my door. "He's got to be Earl."

I climbed into the car and watched as Julian jogged around and did the same. He pushed the key into the starter, but again, nothing happened when it turned.

I pressed my lips together. Two more tries, and still nothing.

"What's wrong?" I asked quietly.

"Don't know," he said, trying again.

"Should we call your mom?"

He sat back, dropping his arm. "She left a half hour ago. She'll be almost home by now."

He opened the door and got out to lift the hood. I got out and went around to stand beside him, but the metal pans and black tubes were a mystery to me.

"Scotty and Blake put this thing together," he said, irritation growing in his voice. "They'd know what to do."

"But you know how to work on cars, right?" I studied his face.

"I can change the oil, but I'm a welder," he said, slamming the hood. "I don't know shit about this stuff." He looked around. "And everything's closed."

For a moment, we stood in silence, thinking. The sound of the bay was a quiet whisper not too far away, and I hated his big night ending this way. I was just pulling out my phone to call my dad when he stopped me.

"Hang on." He caught my hand. "Do you know how to pop a clutch?"

My forehead lined. "Do what?"

He pulled me back around to the driver's side. "It's a standard."

"So?"

I watched him open the door and reach inside before standing up again. "So we can get it rolling and then pop the clutch to start it."

"I've never even heard of that."

Julian put his hands on top of his head and looked at me. "Then I'll have to do it. But I'll need you to push."

My eyes blinked my confusion. "You want me to push your car?"

He frowned and rubbed his hand across his eyes. "Look, I'm really sorry about this, but it's the only way we're going to get home at this point. I'll get it on an incline and help you, but I'm going to need you to push it to get it up to speed."

Laughter bubbled in my throat. "You know, this is exactly how I imagined this night going. You and me, hob-knobbing with the big wigs, pushing your car back to Fairview…"

"Dammit, Anna." I could tell he was getting pissed, so I bit my lip, swallowing my laugh.

"I'm sorry," I said, putting my hands on the car. "I will say I sure am glad I changed out of that skirt. Lord knows I wouldn't want to be tripping on my hem while pushing the G-ride."

Julian growled and pulled me to him. Then he pressed his lips against mine in a rough kiss that stole my breath. "Shut up," he said. I held his shoulders, eyes closed, fighting my smile. He pressed his forehead to mine and I met his blue eyes. "Now come on. I'll help get it rolling."

I watched as he put a foot inside and shifted the T-bird to neutral. Then he stepped out again to help me roll it to the sloped drive that led into a strip mall.

"Run around back, and watch out," he said. "When it starts, it'll jerk."

Pushing the car wasn't as hard as it sounded with the help of gravity, and Julian got it started on the first try. I ran and jumped in as he turned the car toward home. Once we were on the road, I scooted over and put my head on his shoulder.

"I'm glad you keep it real," I said, trying again to lighten the mood. "You don't let all that fame go to your head."

His jaw muscle flexed. "You're welcome."

"You know, I really thought you were doing the whole fake breakdown thing." I ran my finger lightly down his flexed jaw, thinking of that awesome kiss. "To make out with me or something."

He exhaled. "Not in the Athletic Center parking lot."

"Maybe once we get home?"

"Yes." He started to relax and slipped his arm around my shoulders. "Definitely."

Chapter 5

My eyes grew heavy as we made our way along the dark country roads headed south. We drove a while in silence, with only music playing, and the next thing I knew, Julian startled me awake.

"Dammit," he hissed.

I jumped straight up in the seat. "What?" Then I saw we were parked in front of my house. Everything was quiet.

"I just killed the engine," he said, banging the steering wheel. "There's no way I'm getting it started again."

He turned the key and the starter simply made noises without engaging. "If it was the battery, it wouldn't make that sound. Something more is wrong."

"Just spend the night here," I said, pulling his arm. "You can sleep on the couch. Mom and Dad won't care, and maybe Dad can look at it with you tomorrow."

He glanced up at my dark house. "I don't know..."

"What else are you going to do?" I scooted over and opened my door. "Walk home? Mom would have a fit."

Julian followed me inside, and I went to the closet to pull out blankets and sheets. He helped me make up the couch, and I grabbed a pillow for him to use. Once the bed was made, I rose to my tiptoes and kissed his lips.

"Text your mom. I'm going to bed," I said as he caught my hands. Then he grabbed me by the waist and pulled me to him for a better kiss.

My fingers traveled to his shoulders then into his soft, dark hair. His warm lips parted mine, and our tongues curled together, sending chills flashing all the way to my toes. My fingers tightened on his neck, and he held me closer against his chest.

"I'll be up in a minute," he said against my lips.

My protest disappeared in another hot kiss, and I considered the possibility. Sure, Mom and Dad would wig if they caught him in my bed, but with his mouth pushing mine open and our tongues entwined, I didn't care. I imagined sleeping with him, our limbs following our tongues' lead...

Then he abruptly pulled back. "You'd better head up before I forget your parents are in the house."

I leaned in for one more quick kiss before whispering goodnight and jogging quietly up the stairs. My overheated body certainly didn't have a problem forgetting about my parents. I heard Julian softly call my name as I got to the top, and I stuck my head back down.

"Still my angel?" he whispered.

"Mm-hm," I nodded, smiling.

In my room, I quickly changed and slid between the sheets. I was so tired, I didn't even turn on the lamp and in an instant I was asleep. It seemed like I had just closed my eyes when I felt a gentle touch on my cheek.

I jumped awake with a little squeal. "Julian!"

"Shh!" he said, lightly putting his fingers to my lips.

My heart was flying seeing his dark figure kneeling beside my bed. "You scared me to death," I whispered.

"I'm taking off."

"What?" I frowned, sliding out of the bed to the floor beside him. I was only wearing a sleep shirt and panties, but in the dim light, I didn't think he couldn't see.

He cupped my cheek in his hand and gave me a soft kiss. "I can't sleep. I'm heading back to my house."

"But how? Your car..." Then my eyes narrowed. "Were you really faking all that?"

"No way," he chuckled, and his hand slid down my arm. A little shiver moved through me. I liked having him in my room like this, even if it made me a little nervous.

"I'll walk," he whispered. "It's not so far, and I'm all keyed up anyway."

"Julian!" My fingers quickly closed around his arm, holding him still. "That's at least ten miles! You can't walk that far in the middle of the night."

He exhaled. "I'll be fine."

"But what if you got mugged? And how will you get your car back?"

"Pick me up in the morning." He kissed my cheek and started to stand. "Listen, Anna, I'm totally wired. I can't just lie downstairs in the dark staring at the ceiling. Climb back in."

He held my blankets up, and I slipped between them. Then he leaned against the bedside so our faces were close together. "Now get some sleep," he whispered, kissing my nose.

I propped up on my elbows. "Please tell me what's wrong."

He shook his head. "It's probably just coming down after tonight. You know."

"Probably?" My hand returned to his arm, and I rubbed it up and down.

He was quiet a few minutes, then he started. "I was just thinking about everything that happened and me and who I am and what this is all about." He paused.

I wasn't sure if he'd continue, but I hoped... "And?" I said softly.

"And I'm nobody, Anna." His voice was different. An edge was in it I'd only heard once before. "All these people are making this big deal about me, and what if they're wrong? What if I've had all the great ideas I'm ever going to have? They want more, but I don't have a single idea of anything new I'd like to do. I feel like... like that car out there. Stalling."

For a moment, I was quiet. He didn't say anything more either, and the only thing in my brain was one thing I'd promised to keep secret.

I pulled his hand to my lips and kissed it. "I can tell you two things," I said. "You're not 'nobody.' For starters, look at your mom. She was an amazing artist back in the day—"

"And she quit. Why? Am I just doing the same thing?"

I bit my lip. I knew exactly why she'd quit, and it had nothing to do with her talent. Or his. Taking a deep breath, I said the only thing I could. "You probably *are* still coming down from tonight."

He exhaled and shook his head. "I know, I'm being stupid."

"You're not," I cried in a whisper, sitting up fast and hugging my arms around his shoulders. I felt his hands go to my waist. "Tonight was a huge deal, and your funny car. C'mon, Julian. People have car trouble all the time."

He kissed my neck briefly, pulling away. "I know. You're right."

"And you're always having creative ideas," I continued, not letting him go. "It's the way you're made. What about the bay? You drove me all the way into Fort Spain just to turn around and show me a colorful sunset.

Most people would drive right past that and not even look. You're different. You're special."

"Yeah, I'm so special. I don't even know who my dad is."

Instantly pressure tightened in my chest at those words. I had to bite my lip to keep from exploding. Now *I* was mad. I slid out of the bed again onto the floor in front of him and pulled him into my arms. We held each other in silence several moments while I listened to our breathing and considered just telling him the truth. Forget what his stupid parents wanted, forget my promise. Julian could *not* feel this way to ease their selfishness.

After a few minutes, I took a deep breath and leaned back against the side of my bed facing him. He leaned forward and kissed me, sliding his hand under my shirt to my bare stomach. Warmth followed his touch, and I reached up to hold his cheeks. Then he stood, pulling me up with him, our lips never parting. Tingling warmth crept up my legs as he moved us both into my bed. Our bodies slid between the blankets, and he was partially on top of me, kissing me slowly, gently.

He rose up and pulled his shirt off fast. I only caught a glimpse of the round tattoo on the side of his lined torso before he reached down and slid my nightshirt all the way up, his mouth covering my bare breasts with kisses. I gasped a little noise. Heat roared through my body, following the burning trail of his lips. My hands slid into his hair, as he started on one side then slowly kissed his way to the other, his tongue lightly touching me.

"Julian!" I gasped.

He quickly moved up, covering my mouth with his. Now our bare chests were pressed together, and my heart was beating so hard, I was sure he could feel it. I held onto him tightly. I didn't want him to stop. The feeling of our bodies touching was amazing.

Slowly he released me from the kiss. He wrapped his arms around me, and pressed his forehead into my shoulder. We were both breathing hard, and I lay very still unsure what he would do next. Several minutes passed, and my heart rate slowed. He turned his head to the side, resting his cheek on my chest, but still he didn't speak. After a while, my arms grew tired, and I couldn't tell if he was even still awake. I lightly smoothed his hair with my fingertips until I starting to drift. Then he slid beside me and gently pulled my shirt back down.

"I'm sorry," he whispered.

I pulled myself into his arms and pressed my cheek against his warm skin. "You don't have to apologize."

I didn't realize how protective of him I'd grown until he'd said what he did tonight. I also didn't realize how quickly I would follow him wherever he wanted to take me. I wondered if these new feelings were because we'd known each other so long or if it was because I knew so much about his past. Things he didn't even know. He gently rubbed my back, and I could feel my thoughts twisting into distorted images as sleep pushed against them.

The next time I opened my eyes, it was light outside, and Julian was gone. I heard voices downstairs, so I grabbed my hoodie and stepped into my PJ pants. In the kitchen, Julian sat at the bar with a cup of coffee. I blinked to the couch, and it was messy and slept in. I wondered when he'd crept out of my room last night.

Going to the kitchen, I caught his eye. He looked at me and smiled, and two thoughts hit me at once. First, how amazingly sexy he was, and second, what happened last night in my room. My cheeks went hot with my mom standing right there, and I stepped over to the sink to grab a glass of water.

"Julian said his big night ended in a typical teenage moment," Mom said.

I tensed, unsure which moment she was referencing. "What do you mean?"

"I told your mom you had to push my car," Julian said.

Chills raced down my arms at the sound of his voice. "Oh, yeah. I didn't know how to pop a clutch," I said, taking a long drink of cold water. I needed it.

"You know, that's a trick most kids probably haven't even heard of," Mom said, oblivious. "I remember when it was pretty common. But there were a lot more standard cars when I was young."

She lifted the pot to make more coffee. "Anyway, I told Julian he shouldn't take that as any reflection on his achievement. People have car trouble all the time."

"I told her that was exactly what you said," Julian's voice was right next to my ear as he leaned past me to put his cup in the sink. My stomach tightened at his closeness, and I had to fight the urge to grab him.

He frowned. "Are you okay?" I managed a nod. "I'm going out to see what your dad thinks. Come with me?"

"Sure."

I followed him out the door, but when we got outside, he stopped abruptly. "What's up? You're acting weird."

"I... I just... You seem different to me today." I said.
"Different?"
"Yeah."

My eyes went to his mouth, and I had an overwhelming urge to kiss him. Instead I only studied my hands clasped together at my waist.

He relaxed with a laugh. "It's the whole fame thing. Makes me irresistible to women."

"It's more than that," I said, glancing up.

He gave me a quick kiss. I wanted to hold him longer, but he was already gone again. "Your dad said he'd give me a ride to my house on his way to work. I'll have to hustle, but I can probably change and catch the bus to school. Can you bring me and Scott or Blake back here after?"

I stopped walking as he ran up to my dad who was looking under the hood of the T-bird.

"I'm betting it's the fuel line," Dad said, his head still inside the car. "But your guys probably know this vehicle inside and out if they rebuilt it."

"I'll let 'em know. Maybe they can bring some parts and we can at least get it out of your driveway."

"You're not blocking anything. Don't feel pressured." Then Dad squinted an eye at him. "Just don't leave it here longer than a few days."

"Yes, sir," Julian laughed.

They climbed into my dad's truck and drove away, and just like that, I was left alone in my driveway with all my raging hormones. I sighed and ran back into the house to dress for school. It was early enough that I could make it to Hammond Island before the first bell, and I had a few things I wanted to say to Bill Kyser.

In my room, I stuffed the letter in my bag and ran back downstairs and out the door already planning my speech.

Chapter 6

I'd driven to the Kyser mansion on Hammond Island so many times in the last year, I could do it with my eyes closed. After Jack and I broke up, I'd sworn I'd never go to his house again because it seemed like something bad happened to me every time I did. A lot had changed since I made that vow.

The four-lane road leading up to the secured neighborhood ran parallel to the Gulf, and I gazed out at the turquoise water. Last night was a huge deal for Julian, but still it didn't cancel the anger he felt about his dad—the self-doubt he'd only let me see one other time when he was injured after the car crash.

He didn't know his dad had been there, proud of him, and even connecting him with a big-name gallery owner in Sterling. He didn't know his dad's birthday gift was a big part of the reason he could even make the huge sculptures that were putting him on the map. I hated it.

My lips were pressed into a thin line as I pulled onto Peninsula Drive and circled to the stucco mansion facing Bayou St. John. I passed several other huge homes dotting this stretch of high-priced real estate. If you drew a line due south of where the Kyser house was located, you'd hit Florida before ending up in the turquoise waters of the Gulf of Mexico. I had no idea why the boundary gerrymandered so, but it probably had to do with money. Most everything here did.

Mr. Kyser's silver Audi was the only car parked in the driveway, and I was relieved. I didn't want Lucy to be home, since I hoped to use the letter as my excuse for this unplanned visit. If she were here, it would be impossible to say the things I wanted to say—that Mr. Kyser *had* to tell Julian the truth. Now.

I entered through the side door that was almost always unlocked and scanned the kitchen for signs of him. Surely he wasn't still asleep. It was 7:30, and he had to go to his office. Although, since he owned everything, I hadn't really considered he probably kept whatever hours he pleased.

"Hello?" I called, wandering into the large living room that was lined with French doors looking out toward the bay. The flagstone patio extended east and wrapped around the south side of the house and formed the driveway. I was very familiar with the layout.

"Mr. Kyser?" I called again, but I didn't hear anyone in the house. Was it possible he was outside?

I couldn't decide what to do, so I slowly climbed the travertine staircase to the second floor. I had no idea where the master bedroom might be, but maybe there was a study or some place I could hide the letter and tell him later? It wasn't my first choice, but it was one option.

Lucy's golden-yellow room was pristine and empty. My eyes went to the door next to it, and a lump twisted in my throat. Jack's room. I wouldn't even let my mind go there.

Jerking my chin away, I turned and walked down the long balcony and around to a part of the house I'd never explored. Another hallway led westward to what had to be the master suite. A door at the end of the hallway was ajar, and as I got closer, I could hear a voice coming from what sounded like an individual moving quickly.

"I can't believe you didn't wake me," the voice said. It was a woman's voice, and as I crept closer, it sounded like Ms. LaSalle's!

"I wasn't awake myself," Mr. Kyser said, and I could hear his smile.

Pressing my eyes closed, knowing it was a huge risk, I stepped forward so I could peek through the crack near the door hinges. I had to know if my ears were right.

When I opened my eyes, I saw Ms. LaSalle in the bedroom wearing only a man's dress shirt. Her long, dark hair slid around her shoulders as she hastily collected a slip, pantyhose, one shoe. "Where's my dress?" she asked.

My eyes went wide, and my hand flew to my mouth. Julian was right—his mom was seeing someone... and it was his dad! It was like a car crash. I couldn't look away. They'd clearly spent the night together, but what did this mean? And would they agree to tell Julian now?

"I'm pretty sure I removed your dress downstairs," Mr. Kyser said in a casual tone that sounded exactly like his son.

I couldn't breathe. Carefully I leaned away, pressing my back against the wall outside the door. I was scared to take a step in case they heard me, but I had to get out of here.

"Come back to bed," Mr. Kyser said. My eyes squeezed shut. "You'll never make it home before he leaves for school. Stay and have breakfast."

Thinking fast—on the one hand, if she went back to bed, they probably wouldn't notice me sneaking back out. On the other hand, if she went back to bed...

"I've got to open the store," she said in a frustrated tone.

"For who?" he laughed. "The snowbirds? No one's going to be beating down the door. Come here."

I heard what sounded like movements on the bed, and I freaked. I never expected these two had made so much progress. Still, I should've guessed it. They'd both disappeared roughly at the same time last night from the reception. I hadn't noticed them leave together, but clearly they had.

This new twist gave me hope. If people saw them together, it would force them to tell Julian who his father was. It was impossible not to see the resemblance when Mr. Kyser and Julian stood next to each other for very long.

"What am I going to tell him?" she said, and her voice sounded sad.

I heard what sounded like kissing, and I automatically ducked, holding my eyes and trying to remember if the wooden floor creaked. I had to get out of here. Studying the distance from where I stood to the stairs, I wondered if I should attempt to run.

"Will he ask?" Mr. Kyser's voice was muffled.

"Probably not," she sighed. "But I can't be gone like this. He's still a minor. And... Julian and I don't treat each other that way."

"I know." Mr. Kyser's voice was clearer now, thank goodness. I started to take a step to the side... "Julian's a good kid. I wish..." he paused, and I froze. Instantly my ears sharpened and I moved back toward the door. *Say it. Say it...*

"What?" Ms. LaSalle's tone changed. I bit my lip hoping it wouldn't matter.

Mr. Kyser exhaled, and I could tell he was backing down. *Dammit!* "I'd like him to know he can come to me if he needs anything."

"No." The sounds of movement on the bed let me know she was getting up again.

"Just listen to me for a minute." I stepped forward to peek, and I saw Mr. Kyser reaching across the bed to pull her to him. "Julian's becoming a man. He can't run to his mother every time he needs something. I'd like him to know he has someone he can talk to. Someone he can go to if he gets in trouble."

She shook her head. "Julian does *not* get in trouble. And if this is how it's going to be, I'll have to stop coming here."

He leaned forward and kissed her. I moved to the wall again, my shoulders dropping. He was so close.

"Stop it," he said in a low voice. "You know I'd never go behind your back. But he's my son, Lex. I want him to have whatever he wants."

I couldn't help listening now—I wanted Mr. Kyser to convince her. I wanted him to win this argument so badly...

"He already has everything he wants," she said. "And you've helped us a lot through the years. There's no need for this sudden rush of paternalism."

"It's not sudden." His voice was sharp, and my hands clenched into fists. "I'm sure there are things he needs that he wouldn't tell you about. If anything, he wouldn't want to put any pressure on you. How could he know he can have whatever he wants?"

I nodded, mentally cheering him on.

"If there's anything Julian wants or needs, I'll know." Her voice was just as sharp. "And if it's something I can't get for him, I'll call you. Like always."

I'm sure that's what you'd like to believe, I thought. But that was it. She was clearly calling the shots on this one, and no matter what I said to Mr. Kyser, I'd always be barking up the wrong tree. He'd never cross her, and I knew from reading the journals how long he'd waited for her.

I shook my head, looking down. I didn't think Julian's mom would deprive him of knowing his dad if Mr. Kyser asked her straight out like this, but clearly, I was wrong. Turning to go, I didn't care any more if they heard me. I was so frustrated with them.

Just then, Mr. Kyser said, "Let's not fight."

One glance back through the door, and in that moment, I saw him smoothing her long hair from her face before leaning in to kiss her. Her arms went around his neck, and I saw his hand slip inside the shirt she was wearing. That was it. He was finally winning her back, and I knew after all these years, he wouldn't jeopardize that for anything.

I'd have to figure out another way to approach the problem. At least now I knew where he stood. How much he wanted to know his son. Maybe the two of us could figure out a way to convince her. But how?

That was the million-dollar question.

Chapter 7

I was late for English class, and Summer had taken occupancy of the desk right next to mine. *Great.* I used "paper business" as my excuse for being late and took my seat. Class was already well into the discussion of our literature book.

Summer leaned over. "Want to borrow my notes? You missed the first-half review."

"Sure, thanks." I whispered back.

"I'll be in the library during lunch."

Ms. Bowman walked between our desks, and I started scribbling notes in my notebook. I liked *The Sun Also Rises*, and I had already finished reading it. But I knew our teacher would expect our essays to reflect class discussion. Looked like I'd be taking Summer up on her offer.

My mind wandered for a second back to studying at the Kyser house with Jack. We'd only had half a semester of English together because he was moved into special classes to graduate early. He'd helped me prepare for the SAT, and I'd done really well on it, despite taking it right after our breakup. I thought about his clear blue eyes and his smile, and my heart sank. Shaking my head, I angrily shoved those stupid memories away.

Last night with Julian was amazing. I loved being with him. He was sexy and fun and even better, we'd started as friends. We knew each other so well, and I knew he'd never hurt me like Jack did. The bell rang, and it was a good thing Summer was going to lend me her notes. I hadn't heard a word our teacher had said.

Julian met me on the way to math, and I grinned in spite of myself when I saw him. Maybe in time stupid, sneaky Jack memories would be forever gone from my head and the only daydreams I'd have would be about my sexy artist and how great it was to spend time with him.

"Where were you this morning?" he said. "I waited around."

"Oh!" I had to think fast. I couldn't tell him where I'd really been. "Can you believe I went upstairs and fell asleep again? If Mom hadn't come by, I'd probably have missed half the day!"

His arm was around my shoulder, and he looked down. "I guess I kept you up late. Sorry."

"I'm not complaining," I said, kissing his cheek, thinking of his lips traveling across my body with a little shiver. "Did you find Blake? Is he going to help you?"

"Yeah. We'll meet up after school, if that's okay?"

"Sure!"

Mrs. Harris was waiting outside her class again frowning. Instantly, we stepped apart. This teacher acted like we were in boot camp, and we had to pass her class to graduate. I always sat close to the front, and Julian had taken the seat beside me, although I knew he'd prefer being in the back where Montage and the other guys always cut up.

Actually, he was doing great, while I was having trouble concentrating. Mrs. Harris would talk about solving inequalities, and my eyes would drift over to Julian's hand taking notes. He had long, elegant fingers, and it looked like he was actually working on a small sketch, which didn't surprise me. My eyes floated up to his mouth, and I thought of kissing him. Butterflies filled my stomach, and his lips curled into a grin.

"You're not paying attention," he whispered.

My eyes met his shining blue ones. "Neither are you."

"The addition principal for inequalities is... Miss Sanders?" Mrs. Harris was at the whiteboard, and I jerked around.

"Uh…" I had no idea.

"If a is greater than b, then a plus c is greater than b plus c," Julian answered.

"Thank you, Miss Sanders." Mrs. Harris's eyes slanted at him, and the class snickered.

"No problem," Julian smiled.

Mrs. Harris went back to her lecture, and I rolled my eyes at Julian as I leaned forward and began copying formulas from the whiteboard. If he got a better grade than me, I'd never hear the end of it.

Winter was not super cold in South County, and instead of hanging around inside the cafeteria at the senior table, we usually sat outside in the quad during lunchtime with Brad and Rachel and some of the other football players who made up Brad's crew. Montage had joined the group, and he fit seamlessly in with the other guys. Nothing had happened with regard to the vendetta that had been on his mind that first night, and I'd almost decided Julian was right, it was all a bluff.

Rachel was finalizing plans for the spring dance on her phone, and Julian was sketching a group of students sitting in a line. I stabbed at a pasta salad I'd brought to eat, but I wasn't hungry.

"What do you think of this," he asked, turning the book to me.

"I like it. What's it for?"

"Mom knows this old guy who used to run a wrought-iron fence company." He turned the sketch book back around and continued shading. "He told her I could come over and pick through his scraps, and I was thinking I could make something for that new sculpture park in Newhope."

My eyebrows shot up. "Did I tell you Mom is trying to get you on the rotation as one of the featured artists at the association?"

"I love your mom," he said with a grin. "Would your dad mind if I asked her out?"

"Yes," I said, narrowing my eyes.

Julian grinned at me.

"Hey, Julian, your mom came in the store last week," Wade Ryan, one of the team's biggest linemen interrupted. He worked at the building center in Fairview.

"Really?" Julian's brow creased. "That's weird. What did she need?"

"I have no idea," Wade said, sitting up straighter. "But that is one fine woman."

My back was to Wade, and I made a disgusted face at Julian. He glanced at me and smiled.

"Uh, yeah. Thanks, man." He turned back to his sketch book.

"So where's your dad?" Wade continued. "I'd like to know what the competition looks like."

Rachel slammed her phone down. "Are you being a jerk, Wade?" she said loudly.

"No way!" He laughed. "I'd like to take her out, treat her right—"

"Dude," Brad's loud voice cut him off. "Shut the hell up." Then Brad leaned forward clapping Julian's shoulder roughly. "He gets hit in the head a lot."

I jumped up, pulling Julian's hand. "Oh, god, I almost forgot. I've got to meet Summer at the library." Then I groaned. "Please come with me. You know it's going to be *awful*."

"Sure," Julian said, folding up the sketchbook. Then he glanced back. "Hey, Wade. I'll let Mom know you think she's hot. I'm sure it'll... make her day or whatever."

"Hey, man, I wasn't trying to offend." Brad's words had subdued that idiot.

"No worries," Julian waved. Then he caught my shoulder and leaned into my ear. "I will never tease you about asking your mom out again. Promise."

I breathed a laugh. "You'd better not quit. It makes her day every time you flirt with her."

He released me, and we continued to the library. I thought about Mr. Kyser being Julian's dad and felt that too-familiar frustration of keeping their secret. That would shut stupid Wade and everyone else's mouth. Maybe I'd stop by his office next week after school to propose a strategy for conquering Ms. LaSalle. Once Julian's car was back in operation.

"So what's this meeting with Summer about?" Julian asked.

"I missed part of class this morning," I exhaled. Then I caught his arm. "And then I missed the rest thinking about you."

He grinned. "Something dirty?"

"Of course. And hey, about that dance Rachel's planning. You're my date, right?"

He waved to one of his passing shop buddies. "Aren't I always?"

"Should I dig out my combat boots or will we dress appropriately this time?"

"You'd look great in combat boots." His hand grazed my thigh. "And a little short skirt..."

I caught his wrist and then laced our fingers. "The short skirts again? You love those, don't you."

"Find me a guy who doesn't."

Just then I saw Summer and called out to her.

"Hi, Anna. Julian," she said in her typical burned-out manner. Then she walked over to meet us.

"I really appreciate you loaning me your notes," I said, releasing Julian's hand. "I'll have them back to you tomorrow."

"Sure, no problem." She handed over the papers. "So what in the world were you doing this morning?"

I shrugged. "Just overslept."

"That's funny." Her forehead creased. "I thought I passed you on the road. Headed toward Hammond Island."

Shit! I coughed. "What? Are you sure? Because I..." I breathed a laugh, glancing at Julian's frown. "I wasn't out there."

Her brow was still lined, and she wasn't backing down. "Don't you drive a green Civic? I know it was you. I recognized your hair."

It was a cool day, and I was literally sweating. "There's just no way," I said, laughing weakly. "Unless I was driving in my sleep."

"Whatever," she said with a shrug. "What did you think about the book? For tomorrow we're supposed to write about our favorite scene and why."

"Oh, thanks," I smiled. "I missed that."

"Yeah, you were totally spaced in class."

Julian coughed a laugh beside me, and I glanced at him, shaking my head in disbelief. "I had a lot on my mind," I said.

"So what's your favorite?" she charged on, unfazed. "I liked the part where Cohn got all steamed up in the restaurant about Brett, and then Jake told him not to go all prep school. Or the part about the road to hell being paved in stuffed dogs."

"Those are good ones, I guess." I had what I needed and was ready to go.

"You got that Jake's impotent, right?" she continued.

"What?" I frowned, thinking. "No, I totally missed that."

"I didn't catch it either," Summer went on. "Mrs. Bowman told us in class today. It's the war injury they keep talking about. Why he can't sleep with Brett."

Julian perked up. "What book are you reading?"

"*The Sun Also Rises*," I pulled my copy out of my bag and handed it to him.

"What's this—200 pages?" He pretended to be annoyed. "And you guys are AP? Why are we reading *A Farewell to Arms*?"

"Oh, you'll like that one," I said, but Julian just stared at me. "I mean, if you read it, you'll like it. You should give it a try."

"It's a doorstop," he said.

"It's not that bad once you get into it." I could feel what Jack liked to call my librarian side coming out. Only he called it my sexy librarian side... I froze. *Why was my stupid brain thinking about Jack?* "But it's sad," I finished.

"Um-hm," he said.

Thankfully, the bell rang, and I could get away from Summer and obnoxious, sneaky Jack memories. We said goodbye, and Julian and I started walking back to the building. He was headed to the technology center, and I had American history.

We walked a few steps in silence, and then he stopped. "What was all that about you driving to Hammond Island this morning? That's where the Kysers live, right?"

I shook my head, trying to be convincing. "I didn't! Summer is so weird. I don't know why she said that." He didn't seem convinced, but I changed the subject. "So I'm meeting you guys in the parking lot this afternoon?"

He nodded. "Blake said he'd drive his truck in case we don't get my car going."

"Sounds great," I jumped forward and kissed his cheek. "I told Nancy I'd start at the paper next week."

"We should have it fixed today," he said, catching my mouth with his. "You won't have to drive next Friday."

"Will I have to push?" I grinned, tightening my arms over his.

"Please. No post-mortems."

I laughed. "It wasn't that bad. I found it very... educational!"

"Great. That's exactly how I'd like you to think of me."

I let him go. "See you this afternoon."

I took off for class, thinking about my plan to visit Mr. Kyser's office and strategize. If he and Ms. LaSalle were seeing each other again, I could let him know about the car breakdown and see if that had any influence on their decision to tell Julian the truth.

Then I thought about the Audi Mr. Kyser drove and Will's BMW. Jack said he wasn't into cars, and he drove Will's old Jeep because he preferred a sailboat. But even

Lucy had a new car. Surely Julian's dad would spring for something reliable for his other son.

But it was more than cars, I thought, my brow creasing. I saw how it stung when Wade made that crack about Julian's dad. It hurt me seeing Julian's face. I had no idea what it would be like to grow up without one of my parents—without even knowing who he or she was. Clearly, it bothered Julian, and from the tone I heard in Mr. Kyser's voice this morning, it bothered his dad, too. We had to get through to Ms. LaSalle.

Chapter 8

Blake Fausak was a big guy with light brown hair and a friendly disposition. He was also a pro at fixing cars, and Julian and I sat back and watched as he skillfully took the T-bird apart piece by piece at my house.

"Seen that new Lexus?" He happily chatted as he worked. "LFA? Zero to sixty in three point six seconds. It's their flagship model now. Four hundred thousand dollars."

"That's crazy," Julian said, twirling a socket wrench. He looked at tools as potential *objets d'art*, and I absolutely loved him for it. "Who spends that kind of money on a car?"

"Man, I'd love to get my hands on one," Blake continued. "Light, too. I read it's a little over three thousand pounds. Got a V10 engine."

"What's it made of?" That got Julian's attention, and I tried to listen and learn, although I didn't plan to suggest his dad buy him a four hundred thousand dollar car.

"They started with some spaceage aluminum," Blake went on. "But switched over to carbon fiber."

Julian nodded.

"Think you could work on that?" Blake asked.

"Probably," Julian said. "You think they'll get one at the showroom in Sterling?"

Blake snorted a laugh. "Doubtful. But maybe. I'll check on it and we can get dressed up and see if they'll let us give her a test drive."

Julian laughed. "Think we can beat them to the border?"

"With 552 horsepower?" Blake cried, pulling out another tool. I was clueless as to what he was doing. "No sweat. You like margaritas, right?"

"Tequila," Julian answered.

Blake continued working a moment in silence.

"Hey, Blake," I jumped in. "What's your ideal car? Like if you could drive anything?"

"Anything?" He pulled out a hose and examined it.

"Within reason," I added quickly.

"Hmm... probably a BMW 3-series. That is a sweet ride."

"Really?" My brow creased. "Why?"

"Just a good all-around car," he said, bending the black hose and looking closely. "Positive steering, rear-wheel drive, fast, but decent gas mileage. And it looks... so fine."

At that last part, he looked up, and his eyebrows rose. His face took on a dreamy expression, and I grinned. "I'll have to start paying more attention."

"Okay, here's the problem." Blake showed us the hose that even I could tell was bad. "Fuel line. You're lucky you made it home. When this goes, nothing happens."

"Got what you need to fix it?" Julian asked.

"Yep, hang on." Blake walked back to his truck, and I looked over at Julian.

"Dad was right," I smiled.

Julian leaned over and bumped my shoulder with his. "Your dad knows more about cars than I do."

I bumped him back. "I bet even a four hundred thousand dollar Lexus won't run with a bad fuel line."

His brow relaxed, and he kissed my head. "You're sweet," he breathed. "Angel."

Blake had the car fixed in less than an hour and then took off. Julian stuck around a few extra minutes to thank Dad and kiss my nose before taking the T-bird back to his house in Dolphin Shores.

It was late, but I had time to run upstairs and finish copying Summer's notes after dinner. Mom stuck her head in and said goodnight before going to bed. "Hey, hon," she said. "How's it going with Julian?"

I dropped my pen. "Great!" I jumped up smiling. "He's taking me to the dance next Friday if that's okay."

"Just like last fall."

I laughed. "I guess Julian's my date to every dance this year."

"You met Jack at the dance last fall, didn't you?" she asked.

"Sort-of." I couldn't figure out where she was headed. "I actually met him at his house the night I went to study with Lucy. But he was in my English class, so I'd been seeing him before the dance."

"It seems like it wasn't so long ago," she said, looking down. "Have you had enough time to get over that?"

My brow creased, and I thought about the picture Lucy had given me for Christmas. It was of Jack and me at that first dance, and it used to be under my pillow. But I'd stuffed it in my drawer a while back. I hadn't looked at it in forever. Seeing Jack's face still stung a little, but I was determined it didn't.

"I think so," I said, trying for humor. "Jack only sneaks into my brain when I'm not prepared."

Mom came over and sat beside me on the bed.

73

"Sweetie. You need to give yourself time to recover before starting something new."

"Well," I exhaled. "I sort-of suggested we take it slow before Christmas. But now, I don't know. It feels like school's ending, and... I don't want to waste time."

Her eyes were concerned. "But do you still have feelings for Jack?"

I shook my head. "I don't," I said. "Trust me, Mom, I really like Julian. *Really*. And, well, Jack broke up with me. I've got to let him go."

She didn't look convinced, and I couldn't figure out what else to say. "It's just so easy being with Julian," I tried. "And he makes me feel good. I mean, we know each other so well, and the way we talk, it's like... I don't know."

She patted my leg. "Just keep a handle on your feelings."

"That's what I've been trying to do." I said.

She kissed my head and went to the door. "Don't stay up too late."

I finished copying Summer's notes and changed into my nightshirt, but my dumb conversation with Mom... Before I climbed into bed, I stopped at my desk and slid the top drawer open. The picture of Jack and me together greeted me like an unwelcome intruder. It was the first time I'd looked at it since moving it from my nightstand to my desk, farther away from me, on its way to my closet. His perfect smile and bright blue eyes still made my stomach hurt. I remembered his kiss, the feel of his hands, me sliding his blond hair back with my finger...

Like an idiot, I wondered what he was doing, and if what Lucy said about him not dating anyone was true. My stupid eyes actually got warm.

"Ugh!" I growled, slamming the drawer shut. Even if what Lucy said was true, I didn't care. We broke up, and he didn't say we were waiting for each other. We *weren't* waiting for each other. *I* wasn't waiting.

I was pissed now. That old memory left me feeling heavy, and I was about to crawl under the covers hoping I wouldn't cry when I heard the faintest tapping sound on my window. I froze, glancing at my clock — 11:35.

I heard it again and tiptoed over to the window, easing back the sheer curtain not knowing what to expect. *Julian!* I reached up to unfasten the lock and silently lift the glass.

"You keep scaring me," I whispered. "What are you doing here?"

He was sitting in the giant live oak tree right outside. "Mom left again," he said. "Can I come in?"

"Hang on," I whispered.

I crept over and turned off my lamp, then cautiously opened my bedroom door. I could hear my dad snoring down the hall, and I closed the door again, turned the lock, and tiptoed back to the window. He was still sitting there, waiting.

"If Mom or Dad catches you, they'll lose it," I said.

He looked down. "Okay — I'll take off."

"Wait," I said, remembering falling asleep in his arms last night, how good it felt. His lips on my skin. "I mean, you can come in. But just be quiet!"

He grinned and climbed through, dropping softly to the floor. I sat facing him. We looked at each other for a few seconds. I wasn't sure what to do.

"What were you thinking?" I finally said.

"I don't know." He reached for my hand. "I heard Mom leave, and I was just lying in my bed all alone in that house. I thought I'd come see if you were still up."

"You're lucky I had to copy Summer's notes and do that assignment." I let him lace our fingers. "Or I'd have been asleep."

His blue eyes flickered to mine, and it was all I could do to stay where I was. "Would you have got up and let me in?"

"Yes." I didn't hesitate.

We stood, and he followed me to the bed. "I thought about following her tonight," he said. Then he let out a brief laugh. "It's so weird. I kind of really want to know what she's doing."

That idea was intriguing. What would happen if Julian caught his mom going to Bill Kyser's house?

"Maybe you should follow her," I said.

"Yeah, but then what?" he sighed as I turned back the blankets. "I guess she'll tell me when she's ready."

"She should tell you now." I sat on the bed facing him. "Who do you think it is?"

He slipped the long-sleeved flannel shirt he wore off his shoulders as I watched. "I don't know. When Wade said that today about her being at the building center, I thought maybe it was some guy he works with."

"Somebody like Wade?" My brow lined as I admired his physique, standing there in only a white tee.

He sat on the side of my bed, pulling off a Chuck. "That would be..." he breathed a laugh. "Unexpected."

"Well, it's not," I said, shaking my head.

"What?" He frowned, pulling off his other shoe.

I jumped, trying to cover. "I mean, I'm *sure* it's not. Somebody like that, I mean."

We sat for a few seconds facing each other. I couldn't help it—I had to cover a yawn with my hand.

"You getting tired?" he asked, pushing one of my curls back.

"It's almost midnight."

"Get in," he said, standing up. "I'll sit beside you til you fall asleep."

I stood and stepped into my bed. Then I stopped. "You want to climb in for a few minutes?"

He grinned and slid in behind me. "I was hoping you'd say that."

I turned so my back was pressed into his chest. One of his arms went around my waist, and the other was under my head. I felt him kiss the top of my shoulder, and warmth flooded my body.

"Will you fall asleep?" I asked.

"Probably." His breath against my neck tingled my skin. "But I can set my phone to vibrate early."

He took his arms away, and I scooted around to watch him set the alarm. He slipped it in his back pocket and looked at me.

"It's nice being here with you," he said, stroking my cheek with the back of his finger.

"I like you being here with me."

He cupped my cheek and kissed me softly. I kissed him back, and he rolled above me kissing me deeper as I wrapped my arms around his neck. I felt his hand slide slowly down the front of my nightshirt. My heartbeat picked up, and I slid back.

"Wait..." I whispered. "I... I mean, are you sure?" I hadn't told him it would be my first time, and I was actually kind of afraid to tell him after how Jack had responded to the news. Jack had completely shut down and taken me home. It was about the most humiliating thing that had happened while we were together.

"I mean, Mom and Dad are right there," I finished softly.

He looked at me for a second and then nodded, lightly kissing me again and resting his hand on my stomach. "I can wait."

I rolled so that my back was pressed into his chest again. He was softly stroking my arm, and I could feel his warm breath on my neck. It was the best I'd ever felt in my life, and I was just starting to drift when I heard him whisper. "What was your favorite part of the book?"

My forehead lined. "What book?" I whispered.

The Sun Also Rises," he said, nuzzling against my shoulder.

Chills skittered down my arms, and I laced my fingers through his, thinking about my homework assignment. I'd forgotten he'd heard it.

"The part where Brett leaves Jake's apartment early in the morning, and he's watching her walk away, up the street."

I could feel Julian's brow furrow against my skin. "I thought he was impotent."

"He is, but they're in love. She keeps coming back to see him, and they kiss each other and they want to be together, but they can't. They keep trying to play it off like his injury should be funny."

Julian lifted his head, and in the darkness I felt him frowning at me. "That's your favorite part?"

"No." I breathed a laugh. "Not *that* part. The part I like is when he watches her leave. He's very sad, and he says something like 'It's easy to act hard-boiled during the daytime, but at night it's a different story.'"

We were quiet for a minute.

"When was that written?" Julian asked.

"Right after World War I." My eyes were heavy. "A long, long time ago."

He nodded. "It's still true."

"Mm-hm."

He hugged my middle and leaned forward to kiss me behind the ear. I pulled his hand up to my lips then I closed my eyes and fell asleep warm and not the least bit sad anymore.

He was gone when I opened my eyes again. The alarm was sounding, and it was time to get ready for the day.

Chapter 9

Summer was normal enough about getting her notes back in English class, and I avoided getting sucked into another bizarre cross-examination with her. No telling what she'd seen me do lately.

We all turned in our assignments and had some discussion about them. I thought about my conversation with Julian last night and him sleeping over. I was tired today, but I didn't regret letting him in. Falling asleep in his arms was heaven. He caught up with me on the way to math.

"You look tired," he said, lightly resting an arm across my shoulders as we walked.

"I've had the strangest two nights," I said, slanting my eyes at him. "Something keeps waking me up."

"Maybe you'll get better rest tonight," he said.

I frowned. "I'm not complaining."

He grinned, catching my waist. "Hey, I was thinking I might borrow that book when you're finished with it. You've got me interested."

I pulled it out of my bag. "Here you go, and I think you'll like it. It ends at the bullfights in Pamplona."

He held the thin volume, studying it for a moment. "Let me guess. She takes up with a bullfighter."

"*A* plus, Mr. LaSalle. That's exactly right."

His mouth slanted down on one side. "I'm starting to not like our heroine."

I stopped, placing my hands on my hips. "Why? Because she's honest? I'd think you'd be able to relate to her more. She has needs that must be met."

We were quiet for a minute.

"I don't see why his injury has to be such a problem," Julian said. "I mean, they could use their imaginations."

I shook my head. "People were more conservative back then."

We were walking again, and he elbowed me in the side. "Were not."

"Well, either way, it wouldn't have been such a sad story if they'd used their imaginations."

"Why does it have to be sad?" He held out his arms. "If they loved each other, they could make it work. He could keep his lady satisfied."

"Julian," I laughed. "Cohn takes it harder than Jake does, actually."

"What, the prep school guy?" His brow creased, and I couldn't help it.

"You have a great memory!" I cried.

"I just thought what Summer said was funny," he shrugged.

"You should be in AP class with me." I poked his side. "You're very smart. You should challenge yourself more."

"I'm as challenged as I want to be," he breathed, and I couldn't argue with that.

Mrs. Harris was at her door as usual. Julian dropped his arm from my shoulders, and we filed in like good little soldiers.

I was having trouble concentrating again, but I focused on my notebook and tried not to gaze left every five seconds like a moony cow. The most I'd do was glance at his hand, which I could see pretty easily without turning my head. He was usually taking notes as well, but occasionally, I'd see him stray off into a little sketch. I couldn't tell what the subject was.

After school, I drove to the paper office in Fairview. I had the picture from Julian's reception on my digital camera, and I hoped Nancy would let me start writing stories for publication as well. I wanted to build my portfolio to get on my college's paper staff, but I had only gotten one clip last semester.

Nancy was in her office on the phone when I arrived, so I wandered around the newsroom for a few minutes until she was finished. *The Bugle* had been in existence in Fairview since 1907, and the archives were amazing to comb through last year.

Finally she called me in. "How's my best intern?"

I dropped in a chair. "Just stopping by to check in. Got any work for me?"

"Actually, I just got off the phone with Miranda Jordan down at the glass blowing studio in East End Beach?" I nodded. "I was thinking you might do a little piece on it for me. Take some pictures, write it up?"

I almost jumped out of my seat. "Nancy! I was just hoping you'd let me write more this semester!"

She grinned. "I figured I'd stick you on the art beat since you have a connection."

"You're so great," I smiled, getting up. "I'll get started!"

She leaned forward on her desk, then paused. "Oh, and I talked to Curtis about putting in a word for you in New Orleans."

My eyebrows flew up. "And?"

"He said he'd be happy to make a call, but I'll follow up. He'll forget." She turned around and started working on her computer, and I knew she didn't expect it. Still I stepped around her desk.

"Thank you so much," I said, hugging the back of her shoulders.

She shrugged me off. "You're a hard worker, and I use those archives all the time. Consider it repayment."

"If you say so." I went to the door. "Oh, and I've got pictures from that reception for you."

She spun around and stood up then. "Let's see them."

We walked over to the larger computer out front and uploaded the images. The one of Julian with Mr. Kyser and his mother popped up, and my breath caught. I wasn't sure if Nancy would see the resemblance as quickly as I did, not knowing the truth.

"That's a good-looking kid," she said, elbowing my ribs.

"I think so," I smiled.

"This is good." She sent the picture to the photos account and straightened up. "Keep it up, and you won't have to worry about anybody's help. You'll make your own way."

"Thanks. So I'm going to take off. How long do you want the story?"

She waved her hand as she entered her office. "As long as it needs to be. Not too much, but something solid."

"Very specific," I muttered.

"Focus on getting lots of good pictures," she called back. "That'll sell it."

I nodded and grabbed my bag, running out to my car. This couldn't have worked out better. I'd make contact with Miranda and if there was time, I'd stop off at Mr. Kyser's office. It was right down the road in East End Beach.

The glass blowing shop was unexpectedly chaotic. Miranda was wrangling a herd of elementary kids through a "hands-on" painting activity, and paint was flying everywhere. They were creating self-portraits, and the long worktable was divided by a center line of make-up mirrors.

"We tell the parents to dress them for mess," Miranda said. "Sorry, I should've told Nancy to warn whoever she sent."

"I'm not really in anything nice," I laughed, dodging a little boy's backswing.

I weaved through paint-covered fingers and took several shots of little ones recreating themselves on canvas. I got a nice one of Miranda guiding a little hand through a sweeping motion.

Budget cuts had forced the elimination of art classes in several schools, and the small private academies in the area couldn't afford additional art teachers. It was a great service Miranda provided once a week for three hours, and I was trying to decide which angle to take — the importance of early art exposure or the need for additional funding for art in schools. I decided just to take lots of notes and pictures and talk it over with Nancy.

I left the center an hour later surprisingly paint-free and drove straight to Mr. Kyser's office in the Phoenician I building on the Gulf. It had been weeks since I'd visited his penthouse office, and I was dropping in unexpectedly. The letter was still tucked in my bag from my earlier trip to his home. If I didn't make the pass today, I'd have to hide it in my drawer again. It was too risky carrying it around with me. It could fall out or anything might happen.

The receptionist was new, so I introduced myself and asked to see Mr. Kyser. I said he was expecting me and that I was with the paper, but she still made me wait. He had someone in his office, she said.

I had just sat down in the small waiting area when the door cracked, and I saw the back of Will's head. I grabbed a magazine and tried to shrink behind it into my chair, but he stopped and turned back, leaving the door slightly ajar.

"You can blow me off," Will snapped, sounding just as unpleasant as ever, "but if you don't do something, they're going to throw him out on his pampered ass."

"I'm not blowing you off." Mr. Kyser's tone was dismissive. "And lower your voice."

Will's voice did go lower, but not low enough. I could tell he was fuming about something. "He's acting like an idiot. I'm ready to kick him out myself."

"I don't understand," Mr. Kyser seemed distracted. "He's always done well in school. Is it a girl?"

"Not that I've seen. It's not even a frat pack. I never see him with anyone."

There was a brief pause. Then Mr. Kyser spoke again. "Maybe he's not being challenged."

"He's failing," Will snapped. "He doesn't go to class. He's always at some dive in the Quarter or at Fat Harry's. He could at least go to Mr. B's or Galatoire's, somewhere with class and be a drunk."

I winced at his words. They were talking about Jack, and as much as I hated it, worry filled my chest. Lucy had said he was alone. I didn't want him to be in trouble.

"Your brother is *not* a drunk." Mr. Kyser sounded pissed now. "Don't ever say that again."

"Why are you hesitating? Last year, you came over at the slightest hint of a problem. Why are you dragging your feet now?"

Mr. Kyser exhaled, and I leaned forward just in time to see him sit in the chair behind his desk. "I'm not dragging my feet. You're adults. I can't run in and fix your problems all the time. He'll learn from his mistakes."

"Don't give me that," Will sneered. "You always cushion his falls. What's keeping you here?"

"Are you done? I'll deal with your brother. Now I've got work to do."

When Will turned, he spotted me leaning forward and listening. His eyes narrowed, and I sank back in my seat, lifting the magazine I held again.

"I thought we got rid of you," he said, pausing at my chair.

I didn't know what to say. Thankfully, Mr. Kyser appeared behind Will, but he was frowning, too. Now I wished I'd called before I came.

"What do you need, Anna?" Mr. Kyser said.

"I… uh… I'm here about that paper you wanted," I said, hoping nobody questioned me further. I wasn't sure what to say next.

"This is not a good time," Mr. Kyser said, then he gestured to his oldest son. "Do you know Will?"

"Yes." I looked down and clutched my bag closer to me.

"We met last fall at the house." Will glanced at my bag with a frown. "She was hanging on Jack. What paper? Why are you here?"

His words irritated me. He made me sound like a remora. "I work for the city paper. I interviewed your dad last fall."

"I'll be here Tuesday," Mr. Kyser said to me. "Come back then."

Will's eyes narrowed and quickly flicked from his father to me. "What's this about?" he demanded. "I'm not stupid. You don't talk to the paper. And since when do *you* just drop in to see my father?"

"Don't be an ass," Mr. Kyser said to his son. "That's all, Anna. Will, I forgot to show you those plans."

Will hesitated as if he were considering something, then he stepped back into the office and closed the door a little too hard. I remembered to breathe and hurried to the elevator. Mr. Kyser was giving me a chance to get away without having to ride down with his oldest son, and I was happy to take it. But I felt sick from the conversation I'd overheard. Was Jack a drunk? Lucy had said he wasn't dating anyone, and now Will was telling his father he never went to class. I couldn't figure it out, and I couldn't help worrying about him.

Jack had wanted to get to Tulane and finish quickly. It had been his whole reason for breaking up with me—so he'd have no distractions. What could have changed? I drove home puzzled and wondered if I should try calling him. I shook my head. I had to let him go. It was what he wanted, and it was what we'd agreed to do. I'd have to trust his father to take care of him. Jack had always been the favorite anyway. And Lucy would tell me if things got really bad.

Chapter 10

By the night of the dance, I couldn't help noticing the atmosphere among the senior class was changing fast. Kids I'd never paid attention to before were suddenly like old friends, and a distinct sense of camaraderie permeated the group. We were on the launch pad, and everything we did got us one step closer to graduation and to starting our lives. It was as if we were all holding our collective breath waiting to see what would happen next.

After school, I drove to Tamara's hair salon to have my curls blown out. It was Julian's and my first dance as a real couple, and I wanted everything to be perfect.

"So Julian again?" Tamara grinned as she pulled my hair straight with her big round brush. "I knew you'd get back to him."

"I know. You told me so." I flipped through a fashion magazine as she worked. "So you're taking a break from college?"

"Girl, I can't afford it this year." She shook her perfectly styled dark curls. "Have you seen Montage since summer? I don't know what happened to him, but it happened."

"I think he's the biggest person I've ever seen," I laughed.

Her head was still shaking. "You should try feeding him. He must drink a gallon of milk a day. I might have to start charging you full price!"

My eyes flickered to hers, and I thought about my bare account. "But you'll warn me first, right?"

She laughed at that. "Once you get a real job." She continued straightening. "So it seems you went from one fine young man to the next."

"I've always spent time with Julian," I said not looking up. "We've been friends for a while."

"Don't act so innocent. You're turning red just thinking about him."

My lips pressed into a smile. "It's just because you're embarrassing me."

"No need to feel embarrassed." She pulled one of my locks into submission. "It's only natural!"

"I do like Julian, and we are together." I put the magazine down, thinking. "I guess we've been taking it slow."

"How come?" She was nearly finished, touching my now sleek head with a clear liquid.

I shrugged. "I don't know."

Our eyes met and she smiled. "Sounds to me like you're wasting time. You're not getting any younger. Grab that bull by the horns if you know what I'm saying."

I started to laugh. "I'm not sure if I do!"

"You will when it's time."

The white cotton dress I'd picked out to wear was the same one I'd worn last fall to the birthday party disaster. Julian had said he thought I was pretty in it, and I wondered if he'd remember. It was also short, and while I didn't have combat boots, my knee-high black boots were in the same category.

I pulled a thin, black sweater over my shoulders and started for the stairs, but I stopped and went back, grabbing my ring off my dresser. Slipping it on, I admired it for a split second, deciding this night was going to be amazing.

Julian's eyebrows rose as I ran down the stairs, and my stomach tightened. He was dressed in his standard dark jeans and a tee, but tonight he also had on a blazer. As always, he looked so hot.

"I didn't have combat boots," I said, trying not to blush, "But these'll do, right?"

"Combat boots?" Mom frowned.

"Inside joke, Mom."

"Well, I think you both look great, now hold still for a picture."

"You didn't do this last year!" I complained as she caught my arm and positioned us in front of the fireplace.

"I should've," she said. "You could've done a comparison."

I rolled my eyes and we took the picture. "Have fun," she called, and we waved, heading to the car, which started without hesitation.

Julian slipped his hand over to the inside of my knee. "I really like this dress."

Warmth traveled from his touch to every part of my body. "I remembered."

He gave me a little pat, and my mind wandered to how soon we might be alone. I wanted his hands everywhere. "It's going to be a good night," he said.

We made our way through the gym chatting with friends. I saw Montage dancing with Cynthia Williams and gave him a small wave. He smiled, and I imagined Tamara trying to stock her fridge to keep up with him. Wade was on the floor with a junior I'd seen around campus, and I caught sight of Summer. I couldn't tell who her date was—it almost looked like she was with Blake.

Rachel and Brad were together with the spots of the disco light drifting over them. Rachel was pretty as always, in a soft yellow dress and Brad was in his usual khakis and polo ensemble. A photographer was circling the room, and he stopped Julian and me under the canopy for a photo.

My forehead lined as he handed Julian the claim ticket. "Whatever happened to our picture from last year?" I asked.

He shrugged. "It's back at my house."

"You kept it?" I caught his arm, and his eyes flickered to mine.

"It's in a drawer somewhere," he said.

I thought about the picture hidden in my drawer. He pulled my hand up and kissed it, and I wondered if Julian had ever looked at our photo the way I'd looked at that picture of Jack. I wanted to imagine he did as I studied his clear blue eyes. With us it would be different.

"I like you wearing this," he said, straightening my ring.

"I've been afraid to wear it all the time," I said, lacing our fingers. "It's so delicate. I don't want to break it."

He leaned in. "I know a guy who can fix it if you do."

I smiled, thinking of all the things he could fix.

We danced a little longer then visited with friends. Rachel's group was composed of half of the party-planning committee, which made sense considering how much time they spent together. Julian left me to chat with Blake, but I didn't mind as I preferred listening to

Rachel's group arguing prom themes to defending myself against Summer.

When another slow song finally came on, he returned and led me out to the dance floor. His arms wrapped around my waist, and I slid my hands up to his neck. I rested my forehead against the side of Julian's jaw and he leaned down to kiss my cheek.

"Am I coming over tonight?" he whispered in my ear.

I nodded, and we continued swaying to the music. My eyes were closed, and I thought of us together in my bed. I wondered if it was time to tell him my personal secret. I wondered what he would say. If he would freeze up and shut down the way Jack did. My bottom lip caught under my teeth. I'd also decided I wasn't thinking about Jack anymore!

The song changed, and Julian pulled me closer. He slid back the neck of my cardigan and kissed the top of my shoulder, and in that instant, all bad thoughts vanished as a thrill raced from his lips to my toes.

"Maybe I should get you home, so you can get ready," he said.

"Mm-hm." I agreed. Then I realized he was suggesting we leave. My eyes blinked open. "Don't you want to hang out with our fellow classmates a little longer?"

"I can see these guys any time." He led me off the dance floor, and I nodded as he exchanged a wave with Blake.

We were quickly headed to Julian's car when I saw Rachel and Brad in the parking lot ahead of us. They were surrounded by three big guys I didn't know.

"Who's that with Rachel and Brad?" I started to say, but the words died on my lips. I stared in horror as one of the bigger guys quickly raised his fist and slammed it into Brad's face, sending him staggering back. Rachel screamed.

"Get help!" Julian shouted at me, pulling off his jacket and running toward the scene.

"Julian!" I tried to grab his arm, but I missed. He was at Brad's side in an instant—just in time to catch a brutal blow to his side. I screamed as he grunted in pain and doubled over.

For a split second, I thought I might faint. White flashed in front of my eyes. Julian was tall and strong, but he was slim. And as I'd feared, he was no match for the three monsters surrounding them. Even Brad was no match for them. They were clearly football players, and with that realization, I knew who they were—the guys after Montage. I turned just as one of them grabbed Julian's shoulder and slammed his face.

"No!" I screamed, racing to the gym with my heart in my throat. We'd just seen Blake, and I almost bounced off him as I went through the door. He saw the terror on my face, but I couldn't catch my breath. "Parking lot... Julian... Hurry!"

He pushed past me, and I kept going, searching for Montage. I was trembling and gasping for breath when I found him. "Quick—in the parking lot... some guys have Brad and Julian!"

Montage's dark brow furrowed, and he ran toward the exit as did Wade, who'd overheard me. Coach Wilson was following and Mr. Jones, although I knew my ancient science teacher would be little help.

I ran behind them to the parking lot in time to see Montage slamming one of the guys into the side of a parked car. A pickup was throwing dirt and rocks as it spun out in the lot. One of the other guys jumped in the passenger's side and the last one limped and fell into the bed as the truck squealed out onto the dark street.

"They got away?" My voice was a hoarse cry. But I didn't have time to worry about that. I saw Julian dragging himself to a sitting position. His cheek was bleeding, and he was clutching his side as he pulled himself up and leaned his head back against a car tire.

"Julian!" I ran and slid to the ground beside him unable to stop my tears. "Oh, god, Julian."

"Did you see the other guy?" He joked and then groaned in pain.

I shushed him, holding my hand over his mouth. "Is it your ribs? Is it something worse?" He held me back as I reached for him.

"Hang on," he whispered. "That guy's fists were like… cinder blocks."

Brad limped over and sat beside Julian against the car. His face was a bloody mess. Rachel was crying and had gone with one of the teachers for ice and towels. I was still trembling holding Julian's hand.

"At least I look better than you," Julian joked, then immediately clutched his side again.

"That gut wound was meant for me," Brad said.

"I'm starting to rethink this friendship." Julian leaned his head back against the car. "My ribs can't take it anymore."

"You boys sit tight," Coach Wilson was frowning. "I called EMS. They should be here any second. We'll be pressing charges, and we need you guys to give descriptions."

Wade and Montage swaggered up clapping each other's backs.

"I beat the shit out of that dude," Wade said. "Did you recognize any of 'em?"

"Nah, but they were from Crystal Shores," Montage said. "I'd been waiting for something like this."

Brad looked serious. "They just asked if I was Brad Brennan. I said yes, and they started wailing on me."

Montage frowned, thinking. "It doesn't make sense. Why go after you?"

"I don't know, but you got some... ah—guts, Julian," Blake said, glancing at Mrs. Womack, who had just come out to check on the group. I nodded at my former civics teacher.

"Three against one's not a fair fight," Julian replied.

"One of those guys against either of you's not a fair fight." Montage said. He glanced around making sure we were alone again, then his voice dropped. "I'm going to find out who they were and finish it."

"Let me know if I can help," Wade said in an equally low voice.

The guys clasped hands, but Julian exhaled, leaning his head back on the car. "I've got to sit that one out."

Brad gripped his shoulder. "Thanks. Again."

Julian waved him away. Flashing lights appeared around the corner, and in minutes the guys were being inspected by emergency medical technicians. Julian was diagnosed with three cracked ribs and wrapped in gauze and tape. The tech cleaned up his face and put a small bandage and an ice pack on his cheek. Brad's wounds were primarily facial, but they didn't think his nose was broken. Wade's hands had to be wrapped, but he and Montage were otherwise uninjured. Brad's attackers had fled once the big guys showed up and started throwing punches.

The tech dosed Julian with a heavy pain killer and instructed me to drive him home. He was conscious as we climbed into his car, but they warned us the medicine would kick in fast.

"You can just sleep at my house," I said, gripping the wheel hard. "I'll text your mom, but I'm not going to scare her. You can tell her what happened tomorrow."

Julian's eyes were closed, and I wasn't sure he heard me until he spoke. "Huh? Oh, yeah."

He was starting to doze, but we managed to get into my house, where Mom was still up watching TV. Julian staggered over and leaned against the bar.

"You're early," Mom said, getting up. "What's going—oh! What happened?"

I held Julian's arm as I explained. "These thugs jumped Brad in the parking lot, and Julian ran in to help..."

"What?" Mom's face was horrified. "Were they arrested?"

My jaw clenched. "No. But the guys think it was a football player after Montage, Tamara's little brother—"

"I don't understand." Mom shook her head. "Why is someone after Tamara's little brother?"

Julian looked like he was about to fall over. I slipped under his arm and tried to help him walk, but he was too heavy. "A vendetta? Montage hurt him in a game? Only he says he didn't. I don't really understand what happened or if it was even connected, but they gave Julian painkillers. I thought he could sleep on the couch."

"Why didn't you take him home?" Mom exclaimed, taking Julian's other arm. "The couch is so uncomfortable!"

"Because... then I'd have to leave him..." I couldn't hold back the tears any longer. I tried to stop, but I was sobbing. My shoulders shook, and Julian came around.

"Whoa, whoa," he said, pulling me into his uninjured side. "I'm good. I just need to... take a break."

I fought to regain control. We were losing him fast. "Maybe Julian could sleep in my room, and I could take the couch?"

Mom nodded. "Sure. I'll help. But hurry."

The three of us made it up the stairs, and I ran ahead to turn back my bed. Julian was almost out before we managed to get his shoes off and secure him under the blankets.

"He'll be fine," Mom hugged me. "Just let him sleep."

I inhaled a shaky breath, my eyes growing warm again. "It was so awful," I whispered. "Those guys were twice the size of him, and they were just beating him..."

I shuddered at the memory, and she squeezed me again. "He's pretty resilient. Remember last year?"

"I try not to," I said recalling the car wreck that had left Julian unconscious and hospitalized. "I'm going to hang out in here and read or something. Just to make sure he's okay."

"Okay." She let me go and went to the door. "Don't stay up too late."

I grabbed my sleep shirt and walked across the hall to change and wash my face. When I returned, Julian was sleeping deeply, and I closed the door. My parents' light was out, so I slipped in behind him and put my arms around his waist. He stirred slightly before falling asleep again. The next time I opened my eyes it was daylight. Julian was still asleep, and for a moment, I simply held him. It felt good knowing he was here and he was safe. I listened to him breathe and let my body relax.

Then I remembered my parents. Quickly sliding out of the bed, I tiptoed down the stairs. Mom was in the kitchen making coffee, so I stopped creeping.

"I guess I fell asleep," I said.

"You looked pretty cozy." She gave me a look, but immediately softened. "I'd fuss, but I saw how gone he was when we put him to bed."

"Whatever they gave him was really strong." I picked up a mug and got some coffee. "He's still sleeping."

"Probably for the best," Mom said with a nod. "Cracked ribs are painful."

I nodded, sitting at the bar.

She leaned forward across from me. "That was a terrible thing. Are you okay?"

"I'll be okay," I said, sipping my warm drink. "And we were having such a good time. I only thought about Jack once when the photographer—"

"You thought about Jack?" Her face pulled into a frown.

I shook my head. "I don't know why I said that. It was because we just talked about it..."

But it was too late. Mom's eagle eye was on me. "Have you been thinking about Jack other times?"

"That's not what I meant. I never think about Jack when I'm with Julian." I let out a short laugh, wondering what was wrong with me. Clearly, I'd been around Summer too much. She was rubbing off on me.

Mom walked over and put her arm around my shoulders. "Break-ups are hard, and you're so young. I'm really sorry, honey."

Just then I heard a noise on the stairs and saw Julian making his way down gingerly. "I can't tell which is worse. The ribs or the hangover," he said.

"How did you sleep?" I went to him and held his arm, which he carefully lifted around my shoulders.

"I don't remember much," he said with a wince. "Were you with me?"

"Yeah. I fell asleep."

He held out his free hand. "Mrs. Sanders, I swear…"

Mom laughed, shaking her head. "You were almost incoherent when we put you to bed last night. But don't get any ideas."

"The next time you take narcotics, we're sleeping at your house," I teased.

My mom gasped, "Anna!"

But I just laughed, going to the kitchen to get him a coffee.

"She's completely out of control, Mrs. Sanders." Julian shook his head as he sat at the bar.

"So, changing the subject," Mom narrowed her eyes at me, "I mentioned this to Anna, would you be interested in being a featured artist at the association in Fairview?"

He reached across the bar, taking her hand. "I promised Anna I wouldn't ask you out, but this might be love…"

Mom laughed, "I'll take that as a yes."

"Just tell me what I need to do and when. It'll probably be at least a month before I can start anything new now," he breathed, getting off the stool again. "And thanks for putting me up. I'd better get home. I didn't check in with Mom."

"I texted her," I said, hurrying over to help him. "Can you drive?"

"I think so," he flinched again. "It only hurts when I move. But I'll take it slow."

We walked outside and stopped at the car. Julian leaned back against it and carefully pulled me to his chest. "Last night did *not* go the way I planned it."

I softly hugged him back and lifted my face for a kiss, but his eyes were looking up and behind me.

"What?" I asked, looking over my shoulder. All I saw was the tall tree outside my window.

"Just thinking about what I can't do now," he said.

My heart sank as I looked back at his face. "How long?"

"Last year it seemed like forever," he said, wrapping his arms over my shoulders. "A month?"

Then he laughed at my expression. "Don't look so depressed. We'll still see each other every day."

"I know. It's just…"

"Different at night?" He shook his head, leaning up and opening the car door. "You've got it easy. I'm the one home alone."

"Maybe I can come to you?"

His lips pressed together, and he shook his head. "I don't know. We'll see how it goes."

"Call me?"

He nodded and kissed me, and I was completely miserable. I hated thug football players with everything in me, and I hoped Montage and the guys found them and pounded them into the turf.

Chapter 11

The incident at the dance had gained notoriety by Monday, and Brad's father was at school first thing demanding answers and increased security. The front office was bombarded with parent calls and members of the community were meeting in droves to discuss safety issues. Blake joined our group at lunch, and he, Wade, and Montage talked about an upcoming visit to our new friend's old campus dance.

"You just stay back and let us handle it," Wade said to Brad at lunch.

Brad had several bandages on his nose and face, and he kept flexing his hand. "I couldn't help if I wanted to."

"This is a bad idea," Rachel said, holding Brad's arm. Their public displays of affection had gone through the roof since Friday. "You should let the police handle it."

The guys ignored her. "Think you'd recognize any of them if you saw 'em again?" Montage asked.

Brad shook his head. "I don't know. I was kind-of distracted at the time."

Rachel took Brad's hurt hand and started rubbing it. "I'd recognize them."

"Too bad you won't be with us," Wade laughed, straddling the concrete bench. "How's it hangin Picasso?"

"Painful," Julian said not looking up. He was working on another sketch, although he couldn't do any lifting until he healed. "Sucky, painful déjà vu."

"I miss you sneaking in," I said softly, bumping his leg with mine. He glanced at me with a smile.

"Were you lonely?" I said. "You could've called."

He shook his head. "Mom was home all weekend. I think she was worried about me."

I nodded, wondering if Will had spent the weekend on Hammond Island. I wondered if Julian's dad knew what had happened to his youngest son.

"You in?" Montage asked Julian.

"Nah," he said. "It hurts to move around too much."

"We'll get in some hits for you," he said holding out his fist. "Honorary member."

Julian tapped his fist back. The bell rang and we started for class. Julian walked slowly with me a few steps before we had to part. He was unusually quiet.

"Are you going to the doctor?" I asked.

He shook his head. "I can deal with this. Done it before."

I nodded. "You okay?"

"Sure," he said. "Just thinking about losing time. Maybe I'll try painting again."

"I think that would be amazing!" I caught his arm. "I'd love to watch, but I've got to get that story to the paper this afternoon. Talk later?"

"I'll call you."

I stepped forward to hug him. "I know it's not smart, but I hope they get those guys," I whispered in his ear.

He smiled and moved a curl from my face. "Take it easy."

"You, too."

By Tuesday, I was more than ready to visit Julian's dad after school. I'd forgotten the letter in my small drawer with all the excitement, but I was going anyway. I had a few other pieces of information to share with

him, and we could set up another time for me t(
the last bit of evidence.

I arrived at the penthouse floor of Phoenician 1 at six, and the new receptionist was gone for the day. No one else was in the office, and I walked over to his door and knocked. It opened slightly, and I heard him on the phone. His back was to me, and he was looking out his wall of windows.

"Bryant told me what happened. Is he okay?" Mr. Kyser said. He waited, listening to the other person. "He needs to get checked out. Send him to my doctor, and I'll put the money in your account."

He had to be talking to Ms. LaSalle, so I kept quiet.

"He's a brave kid. Bryant said Brad was pretty messed up." Something she said made Mr. Kyser laugh. "Yes. Shouting, making a scene, demanding round-the-clock security. Mother hen."

He paused. "Well, Brad's his friend. He couldn't just stand by and watch—"

I figured Julian's mom was complaining about him getting hurt. I agreed with her. Let the football players fight their own battles. Leave him out of it.

"Okay, okay. Who's overreacting now?" His voice was so gentle when he spoke to her. He stood and looked at his view of the Gulf. It really was a beautiful office. "Will's back in New Orleans. I'll pick you up tonight."

Just then he turned and saw me in the doorway. Gentleness gone. "Someone's here. I need to go. I'll see you in a few hours."

He swiped his phone. "Do you have it?"

"No," I shook my head and looked down, away from his frown. "I forgot it at my house, but I wanted to talk to you anyway."

105

"About what."

"Julian?"

Mr. Kyser went back to his desk and sat, then he motioned to the chair in front of it. "What about him."

I walked forward and took the seat. "Well, I just... you'd asked me to keep you posted if he needed anything."

"That situation's changed," he said, lifting a silver pen off his desk pad. "I'm not as out of the loop as I was then."

His reconciliation with Julian's mom was to thank for that, I knew. I decided to let it go and cut to the chase. "Have you thought any more about telling him the truth?"

"We've discussed that enough," he said with a deep exhale. "I'm sorry you found out, but I would expect you to understand my position now, knowing the whole story."

"I do," I said quietly. "You don't want to lose her again."

For a moment I saw the wall come down behind his eyes, then just as fast it was back in place. "Alex has her reasons for waiting."

Placing my hand on his desk, I studied my ring. "Remember the night of the reception?"

He nodded, "Of course."

"I was Julian's date, remember?"

With a loud sigh, he leaned back in his chair. "What's your point?"

My eyes went to his. "Well, after everyone left, I had to help Julian push his car to get it started."

That got the response I wanted. "What?" His brow furrowed, and now he was listening. I'd touched his pride.

"His car wouldn't start," I repeated, my eyes back on my ring. "We had to push it to get it going."

Mr. Kyser's jaw clenched, but he didn't speak.

"He ended up staying at my house that night. He was so angry, and he said some things…" I looked at his dad then. "He needs to know the truth. Your secret is hurting him."

He turned back to the windows, answering slowly, thoughtfully. "I'm very proud of Julian."

"You should be." My voice had grown louder. "He's great, and I'm not just saying that because we're dating."

"Look," he swiveled in the chair again to face me, giving me that old, stern look. Only now I wasn't afraid of him. "I'll speak to his mother again, but that's all I can do. It's her decision."

I nodded and looked down. "You asked me to tell you if he needed anything. Now you know."

I wanted to tell him more, but I couldn't. I couldn't say I'd been in his house the morning he'd argued with Ms. LaSalle, and I agreed with him. That he was right, and there were things Julian needed from a dad. That Julian simply *needed* a dad. Frustrated, I had to figure out another way. Maybe I could try and talk to Ms. LaSalle at some point. I wondered if I could catch her alone at the store.

Mr. Kyser stood as if ready to end our meeting. "Thanks for telling me about the car," he said. "I did ask you to tell me these things. Maybe I can help with that at least."

"He deserves more," I said, meeting his blue eyes.

"I'm sorry. That's the best I can do."

I left Mr. Kyser's office and went to the elevators. The doors opened, but as I was getting on, I heard his voice and stopped. "Anna?"

"Yes, sir?" I looked back to see Mr. Kyser standing out in the foyer.

"Is Julian... interested in cars?" He rubbed his palms together. "I mean, has he mentioned any one in particular?"

I thought for a second. "BMW three series."

"That's what Will drives." He turned his head, eyebrows pulled together. Then he nodded. "Thanks."

I let the elevator doors close and couldn't stop the sneaky grin from crossing my lips. I couldn't wait to see how that played out.

Later that night, I was getting ready for bed when the house phone rang. I snatched it quickly. Mom and Dad were already in their room, and I was the only one still up.

"And she's gone," Julian's voice said quietly on the other end. I hated that he sounded sad.

I lay' back on my bed and wondered just how much trouble I'd get in if I got caught sneaking out. A lot. I'd probably lose car privileges, and I needed the car for my newspaper job. I chewed my bottom lip and exhaled. "You're home alone?"

"Yep," he clipped. "What if I just came through your front door?"

I rolled onto my side, sliding my finger over the pattern of my quilt. "I think that's definitely when you'd get caught."

He sighed into the phone. "So what're you doing now?"

"Getting ready for bed. Thinking of you."

"Same here."

My lips pressed together as I studied the ceiling. "How are the ribs?"

"Painful. Mom sent me to this specialist today. Some fancy place on East End Beach with lots of interior design."

I nodded remembering the phone conversation I'd overheard. He'd gone to Mr. Kyser's doctor. "What did he say?"

"Oh, he took a bunch of X-rays and then said I had three cracked ribs."

I laughed. "He's very good."

"Gave me more painkillers, though. Should help me sleep."

Longing twisted a dull ache in my chest. "I miss you."

"Same here." His voice was quiet again.

"Did your mom say where she's going or anything?"

Sounds of him moving were followed by a low grunt of pain. "I don't think she knows I know," he breathed. "She leaves on foot, so I guess he must pick her up somewhere."

I nodded even though he couldn't see me. "Very cloak and dagger."

"Maybe it's not a boyfriend. Maybe she's a trained assassin." His playful tone made me smile. "She's actually in pretty good shape."

"I can see her now," I joined in. "Scaling the side of a building, laser target set on some guy's forehead. She's just pulling the trigger, and —"

He laughed. "I think it's a boyfriend."

I giggled, and then we were quiet again. My eyes felt heavy. "Did you take a pain pill?"

"No, but I should. You getting tired?"

I rolled onto my side, holding the phone as if it were his cheek to mine. "A little."

"What are you wearing?" His tone sent a charge to my stomach.

"You know what I'm wearing," I said as a grin crept across my lips.

"Close your eyes," he whispered.

"Okay," I whispered back, following instructions.

"Now, I'm kissing your cheek," he said in a low voice. "Now your lips..."

"Mmm." With my eyes closed, I could almost feel him doing it. "Julian," I said softly.

"You're in that little sleep shirt that shows your panties, right?"

My eyes popped open as my face flamed red. "You could see that?"

"Oh, yeah. I like that one." That tone was in his voice again, and my body grew warm. I pressed my eyes closed. "My fingers are just at the edge of it. Feel that?" I nodded, which again was silly. He couldn't see me, but I couldn't speak. I was actually feeling it. "I'm sliding my hands under it. Your skin is so soft. I can smell that fresh soap you use. Now my lips are touching your stomach, moving higher, right up to your little—"

"Hang on," I breathed, a little shaky. My whole body was flushed. "You called the house phone. What if my mom picked up?"

"Hi, Mrs. Stanley!" His voice was loud and friendly. "Anna was just having a problem with her shirt."

Hopping of my bed, I walked to my window. "I don't think I can sleep now."

He laughed. "Works, doesn't it."

"Yes." Then I paused. "But it's not the same."

"I know." He exhaled again, and again I heard him move followed by a grunt of pain. "I should let you go. It's late."

110

"Will you sleep?" I lay back on my bed, forehead creased. I considered throwing caution to the wind and driving to his house—journalism career be damned! Instead I shook my head. "Take a pain pill."

"Bad influence."

"Goodnight, Julian."

"'Night."

I hung up and sighed. Then I let out a little laugh, remembering what he'd said. I just might make it through these next few weeks if that was my nightly call. Next time I might not stop him so fast. Next time he'd have to call my cell.

Sliding between the cold sheets alone I shook my head. Nope, I took it all back. Phone calls weren't enough.

Chapter 12

Basketball wasn't nearly as popular in South County as football, but Julian was bored. And I was learning when he got bored, my life got interesting. Friday's game was also a match-up against Crystal Shores High School, and while the guys who'd jumped Brad weren't on the basketball team, it was turning into a grudge match.

Game day was almost too exciting for school. Teachers attempted to go through their lesson plans, but everyone was distracted waiting for the showdown. The last bell rang, and the parking lot was already filling up with additional boosters and parents. The entire football team promised to show up, and I'd heard the coaches talking about calling for backup with crowd control. Two police cars turned into the parking lot as I pulled out.

It was a sell-out basketball game, a first in the school's history, and staff and parents were doubling their efforts to prepare for whatever might happen. I went home to change and get ready. Julian was picking me up in a few hours, and I was nervous and excited and maybe a little scared. I pulled on my jeans and a navy sweater. I fiddled with my hair and makeup until I heard Julian downstairs. It wasn't super cold, but I grabbed a grey scarf as I headed down. It made me look the part of a loyal Dolphin. Julian was not in navy or gray.

"Rah-rah," he grinned as I skipped down the stairs.

I kissed his cheek when I reached the bottom. "You know, if anything happens, it'll be as much for you as for the team."

He frowned. "I don't get it."

Our fingers laced as we headed to the door. "They're including you in their payback."

"Whatever." Julian dug in his pocket for his keys. "I just wish I healed faster."

"Me, too." I smiled as we started for the door.

Dad stopped us. "Some of the parents are concerned there might be trouble at the game tonight," he said. "You two be careful."

I glanced at Julian. "I haven't heard about anything," he said. "And I'm not looking to get more beat up."

"Right." Dad said. "Well, have fun. Let me know how it goes."

We went out to the T-bird, and I thought of my car conversation with Mr. Kyser. It was too soon for him to have done anything, but I wondered what would happen and when. Julian stopped me at the passenger side and turned me around for a real kiss. His warm lips pushed mine apart, and he tasted like mint. I reached up to slide my arms around his neck. His lips moved to my cheek, and I looked in his eyes.

"What was that for?" I said softly.

His hands slid down to clasp mine. "Just don't get the chance as much anymore."

"It seems that way now that we're only together at school." I laced our fingers. "But aren't you excited about the game?"

He shrugged. "You're more interested than I am."

Gently I pulled his arms around me. "Don't you want some revenge?" I rose on my tiptoes and kissed his lips again.

He kissed me back. "It's not even the same team. Those guys are getting what they wanted with all this."

My forehead lined. "What did they want?"

"Attention." He released me, opening the door. "It was a stunt. Why else would they go after Brad?"

I thought about that a moment. "It *was* Montage who had the problem," I said. "And Brad has already decided to go to Tulane."

Julian nodded, and I considered this twist. "So now what?"

"We go and see how it plays out."

I climbed into the car, thinking as he walked around to the other side. "Rachel's headed to Loyola," he said once we were on the road. "Just like you."

"Not yet. I've only applied."

"You haven't heard anything?"

"Nope," I said. "I'm hoping I will soon, though. If I don't, I guess I'll end up staying home and going to Sterling."

"Would that be bad?"

"I guess not. Mom thinks I'll do fine wherever I go. I just… I applied to some really good schools, and it'd be neat if I got into one."

His eyes were fixed on the road ahead. "One in New Orleans?"

"Not necessarily," I said. "I just think it might be my best chance with the paper connection. And it's not so far from home."

The muscle in his jaw moved. "And that's all you're thinking about?"

Turning in my seat, I studied his profile. Our drive had become unexpectedly tense. "What do you want me to say, Julian?"

"Jack's at Tulane." He said it flat out, and my breath caught. I was not expecting that. "Loyola and Tulane are blocks apart. I know the score."

"What?" I gasped. "There's no score! I mean, yeah, that was part of my motivation to apply in the first place, but I really would like to go there."

He nodded, but didn't answer. My throat was tight, and I actually thought I might cry.

"You can't make a big deal about that now." I managed to say. "We weren't together then."

He glanced my way and seemed to relax, pulling me to him in a careful hug. "You're right," he said softly.

After a few moments of quiet driving, me hugged into his side, I felt a little better. I rocked my head back so I could see his face. "What's wrong?"

He shook his head. "I think it's this rib thing. I can't work, I can't be with you. I don't like being at that house alone."

I tucked my face into his neck, hugging him again. "Do you want to skip the game?"

"And see you pout?" he laughed. "No way. Let's go watch Wade and Montage get arrested."

My head snapped up. "You think that's going to happen?"

"I hope not," he said. "But they'd better be careful. Vigilante justice is a bad idea."

The gym was packed when we arrived, and people were spilling out into the parking lot. A group of trucks was parked on one end of the lot with a pack of football players hanging around it. Police cars were prominently situated with the officers standing out front, chatting and looking official.

Additional cops had been hired for the game, and everyone was waiting to see how the players would react to facing each other on the court. The whistles blew, and it looked like both teams were ready to fight.

Out of the jump, players were pushing and reaching high and low. Whistles kept going off and Brazil Lewis, our point guard barely made it two steps before a player was in his face. Wade and Montage were standing with a line of brutes in front of the stands, and the ball was knocked out of bounds, in their direction several times.

More than one near-fight on the court prompted yellow flags to rain down like a Mardi Gras parade, and by the end of the night, the Dolphins had racked up the most fouls of any game played in the last four years. But Crystal Shores couldn't match us for baskets and the Devils left Fairview in defeat.

The players were mollified, and post-game interviewers pulled Brad into the discussion, focusing on his parking-lot beating and the satisfaction he must feel watching his fellow athletes win. Even Julian's mood had improved by the end of the game. He accepted Brad's invitation to a party planned by Mr. Brennan at the Tiki club in Phoenician VI on East End Beach.

When we reached the high-rise, Brad's father greeted us at the door. It was the first time I'd seen him since the car accident, and when we arrived, he seemed particularly interested in Julian. I could tell he'd been drinking.

"You're a good kid jumping in to help Brad like that," Mr. Brennan said, slapping Julian's back. I saw Julian wince, and tried not to smile. "You got guts."

"Brad would've done the same for me." Julian replied, catching the big man's hand and shaking it before he could cause any more discomfort.

"But Brad spends half the year taking hits like that," Mr. Brennan continued. "You're a good man."

Julian nodded. "Thanks."

We tried to pass, but Mr. Brennan held on. "I knew your Mom way back. How's she doing these days?"

At that, Julian stopped trying to get away. "Good," he said. "She has a business on Dolphin Island. You should stop by and say hello."

"I might do that." He looked at Julian for a long second, and then started to say something but stopped. Instead he looked at me. "I don't think we've met."

"Anna Sanders," I said over the music that had started playing loudly.

"Anna, welcome to the Phoenician," he said, shaking my hand. "Best friend and I built these blocks of concrete years ago. Nothing's knocked 'em down yet."

"They're amazing," I said. It was the first time I'd been in this complex, and I was bursting with all I knew about its history. Or rather the history of the people who built it, present company included.

"Julian's mom designed the interiors of all the Phoenicians," he continued. "But you knew that."

"It was in the article Anna helped write for *The Bugle*," Julian said.

"You write for the paper?" Mr. Brennan asked me.

"I'm just an intern, but I hope to do more this year."

"Well, you kids have fun," he said, finally releasing us to greet a group of adults who'd just entered behind us.

"Thanks," I said.

We left, and Julian watched behind us for a second.

"What?" My brows pulled together. "What's wrong?"

"He sure was interested in my mom," he said quietly, turning back. "You don't think he could be the guy..."

I almost laughed. "Mr. Brennan? C'mon, Julian. He's married."

We continued walking through the Mexican-inspired resort. I couldn't help but remember the trip it was modeled after.

"It would explain all the sneaking around."

I stopped, shaking my head. "No. It is *not* Mr. Brennan."

He turned to face me, frowning. "How would you know? He said he knew my mom way back. Maybe he's my dad."

"He knew her because they worked together," I said. "Your imagination is running wild. Besides, you look nothing like Brad."

He grabbed a drink off a passing tray. I quickly checked to be sure the server hadn't noticed. "Mom says I look like her dad," he said, taking a sip.

"No help there." I couldn't believe he didn't see how much he looked like Mr. Kyser. But I guessed if he wasn't looking for it…

"Julian! Glad you're here. I might need protecting." Brad walked up with Rachel right beside him. The boys clapped hands.

"I'm off that gig," Julian laughed. "Do your own blocking. I can barely move."

I stepped over to Rachel and pretended not to notice Brad and Julian lifting two more drinks off passing trays. I was driving us home, it appeared.

"I've never been so happy about a basketball game," I giggled.

"No joke. The fans led the cheers tonight. It was great. Everybody was into it."

"Julian thinks it was all a stunt." I scanned the room for familiar faces.

"Brad said the same thing," she said, picking a fruit kebab out of a passing drink. I laughed, thinking how confused the servers were probably getting.

Just then the rest of the guys arrived, and the music grew louder. Everyone started dancing and celebrating the win.

A few hours passed, and Julian had disappeared in the crowd. I wandered through the laughing bodies looking for him and finally caught sight of him sitting in a corner with Renee Barron. My jaw clenched as I watched her hold her long brown hair back and lean in to talk to him. She was practically sitting on his lap standing up, and I was majorly pissed.

"Hey, we got separated," Julian said, as I approached them.

"I know," I said, trying not to overreact. "I bumped into Blake and then Montage was talking to me. I think he's been drinking a little."

"I think everyone has," he said, leaning into my hair.

"I see you found Renee." I met her very green eyes smirking at me.

"Hi, Anna," she said, and it irritated me that she was so pretty.

"Hi," I said. "How's college?"

"Oh, it's not hard." She slid her shiny brown hair back. "I'm just working on some prereqs before I apply to nursing school."

"You're moving to Birmingham?" I could only hope...

"What?" she laughed. "No. Probably the University of Sterling."

"The Baptist college?" I intentionally sounded as surprised as possible. "Will they let you in?"

"Be nice," Julian said in my ear.

"I was just teasing," I said, pretending to laugh.

Her eyes narrowed. "I can take a joke. Do you hear from Jack much?"

"We broke up," I said through a tight smile.

"That's right," she said, as if she'd forgotten. Liar.

I turned to my date, who she clearly wanted. "Julian, I'm tired. Can we go?"

"Sure." He was still holding my waist. "I said this was your night."

I slipped my arms around his neck, suddenly inspired. "I know you did. You're always so sweet to me." Then I kissed his nose, feeling Renee's eyes burning a hole in my back.

"Let's jet," he said.

I stepped over and hugged Rachel. "'Night, guys. Have fun."

"'Night," Rachel said.

Renee took that opening to step over and run a finger down Julian's arm. "Get well soon," she said like some evil succubus.

"Yeah, thanks," he said. "Bye, guys."

I was furious. She had a lot of nerve flirting with Julian in front of me. And asking about Jack like that. She knew we broke up. I wanted to kick her bitchy butt. My one consolation was remembering how it went down at the hay maze last year. Julian had left her to be with me.

"What was that face about?" he asked as we made our way to the door. "You look like you're about to knife somebody."

I tried to play it off. "I don't know what you mean."

"Mm-hm. I've seen you make that face before." He slung an arm around my neck, pulling me in so he could kiss my head.

"You're not acting this way because of Renee. I don't care about her."

"Well, I hope not," I tried to pull away and keep walking. "I thought we were dating."

"Slow down." He caught my arm and stopped me. "We are."

I looked up at him, and he smiled. "You are too much," he breathed, taking my face in his hands and kissing me.

His lips pushed mine apart, and my insides warmed as my mouth filled with the flavor of strawberry daiquiri. We hadn't made it out of the club yet, and a few of our classmates started cat-calling.

"Idiots," I laughed, pulling his arm. "Let's go."

Julian waved back to the guys, most of whom were still hooting and giving thumbs up signs. As we stumbled out to his car, he draped his arm across my shoulders again. "Thanks for kicking my butt out here tonight. I was in a mood, and this was fun."

"It's understandable." I reached up to thread our fingers. "You're injured and you can't do what you want."

"Let's walk down to the water."

I nodded, following him. It wasn't too cold, and a bright moon glowed in the sky. The waves were all tipped in silver as we walked down and sat on the sand. It was beautiful and magical-feeling.

"I used to do this all the time," I said with a sigh. "I don't think I've been down here once since school started back."

"We've had a lot going on. Come here, beautiful." Julian reached across and pulled me into his arms. He rolled us over so he was partially above me and kissed me deeply, his tongue finding mine, causing my insides to ignite.

I moved my body closer to his, reaching up to hold his cheeks. We were lying on the sand, and his hand slid down to my neck, to my shoulder, and then lower. I reached for it and laced our fingers. He kissed my hand then untangled his, reaching back to my waist for the bottom of my sweater. His hand went under the fabric and up to my bra. My heart was racing as his fingers gently explored the sensitive skin beneath.

"Julian," I breathed, turning my face, my cloudy eyes scanning the dark beach to be sure we were alone.

"What?" he whispered, moving lower to kiss my stomach.

A little noise came from my throat. His kisses were electric, and I slid my fingers into his dark hair. "Aren't you hurt?"

His lips were burning a path higher, and he spoke against my skin. "I'll stop if it gets uncomfortable. Or not, heck."

He covered my mouth with his again, and my stomach tightened. My entire body was on fire. I could feel myself giving in as his leg pushed between my thighs, moving them apart. Maybe this wasn't the ideal location or how I'd imagined our first time going, but I wasn't about to stop him.

Just then a squeak of sand was followed by a light sprinkling of grains on our faces. Julian sat up fast, pulling me with him against his chest. A pair of wobbly classmates laughed as they passed us, oblivious to our presence.

"Ugh," I exhaled, pulling back and wiping sand off my face. "This was not how I pictured our first time."

He smiled and touched my chin. "How did you picture it?"

"Not with you in pain. Or with all these people around."

"I'm not in so much pain."

I continued to my feet, straightening my sweater and dusting my bottom. "Let's go," I reached for his hand. "C'mon."

"I want to stay," he said, not standing. "I want to be with you."

My shoulders dropped. "I want that, too, but... well, the timing isn't right."

He made an annoyed sound. "The timing's never right."

Pain clenched in my chest. I had assumed he'd agree with me. "Why are you mad?"

"Because I love you," he said looking up at me.

I frowned. "And that makes you mad?"

"No, it just... it doesn't seem to matter."

I leaned over and kissed him softly. "It does matter, but we almost got stepped on!"

He put his hands on my waist and tried to pull me back down again, but I resisted. "Anna!"

"What?" Now I was getting mad. "I said let's go. Let's go!"

"Fine." He stood and held out his hand, but I didn't take it. I pushed past him stalking toward the car.

"Will you stop?" he called.

"No." I walked all the way to the car with him following several steps behind me. When I got there, I stood waiting for him at the back.

Julian walked over and stood in front of me. "So that's it?"

"Are you going to give me the keys?" I said, not meeting his eyes. I refused to cry, even though my insides were all tight and achy.

He exhaled impatiently and held the keys up. "Yes."

I snatched them away and went to the driver's side. We drove the whole way to my house in silence—all twenty minutes—and when we stopped in the driveway, I grabbed the handle to get out, but Julian caught my arm. "Why are you acting this way?"

"Because you're trying to make me feel bad."

He shook his head. "I'm not trying to do anything."

"Yes," I said, sarcasm in my voice. "You've been acting normal all night."

"I'm not acting normal, I'm pissed." Even in the dark I could see his jaw clench. "I want to be with you. But you don't have to feel bad. I said what I did, and you said what you did."

"And I feel bad because I don't want to make you mad." Then I looked down and sighed.

He pushed his head back against the seat. "Well, I can't make you say the words."

My brow lined. Suddenly, I wasn't sure if we were talking about the same thing. I thought he was mad because I didn't want to have sex with him on the beach, and I was mad because I had expected him to understand I didn't want our first time to be practically in public with drunken classmates stumbling all around us.

"I don't understand," I said.

"Look, I'm sorry. I love you, and I want to be with you. You don't feel the same. That's just where we are."

I didn't have a response. "I'm confused."

"About what?"

I shook my head. "I don't think what you're mad about is the same thing I'm mad about."

"It's late," he exhaled leaning over and kissing my head. "My side's hurting. I've got to get some rest."

I chewed my lip watching him staring ahead in the dark. "Please don't be mad at me," I said. "I do want to be with you. Just not like that."

"Okay," he said simply.

I wasn't convinced, but I leaned over and kissed him softly. "Are you okay to drive?" He closed his eyes and nodded. "Well, sleep good then," I said.

I got out and walked to the door. I knew we weren't okay, and it made my chest ache like a huge hole had been blown in it with a sawn-off shotgun. But I didn't know what else to do. I stopped at the door and looked back. He was still watching me from the car. I waved and he smiled slightly. I opened the door, as he put the car in reverse.

Chapter 13

The wave of excitement following Friday's game carried over into the next week. Mardi Gras was around the corner, and every day Rachel's school krewe had planned a different spirit activity for the student body. Our school always named a carnival king and queen, and Rachel and Brad were a sure thing to win the title. We'd find out the winners on Friday, and a ball was planned for that night. It was a big, fun weekend, and I was hoping Julian and I would spend it together.

He'd been distant since our argument, and on Monday, he'd said he was meeting up with Blake during lunch—doing some welding on a car Blake was restoring. I didn't complain because it allowed him to pick up the blowtorch and didn't require heavy lifting. I hoped it would help him feel better and get us back on track.

Rachel took a break from decorating and preparing for Friday to run out and give me the latest on her apartment search in New Orleans. "There's an apartment complex on St. Charles Avenue that's just a few blocks from campus," she said. "It faces the street, and I think it'd be perfect. It's not too expensive, and we'd have a doorman."

"That sounds great, Rach!" I said, looking at the pictures on her phone.

"Have you heard any more on scholarships?"

I shook my head. "No, and I'm getting discouraged. It's getting late."

"Well, hang in there," she said, giving my arm a squeeze.

"I'll probably have to get a student loan for what Mom and Dad can't cover."

"I thought of doing that," I said. "But it'd take forever to pay back on a journalist's salary."

"Not if you moved to New York!" she said. Then she turned serious. "What will you do if you don't get it?"

"Shoot myself," I said.

"Anna!"

"I'm just kidding." I sighed. "I'll probably just stay at home and go somewhere local."

"At least you already have a job, right?"

I thought of working at *The Bugle* full-time, and while I really liked everyone there, I'd hoped to get out and live a little before retiring to a smaller paper — or whatever people were reading at that point.

"I guess," I shrugged.

After school, I went to the office. My art center piece had turned out really well. As Nancy predicted, the pictures sold it. She said I was a budding photographer, but it was hard to take a bad picture of those little guys. They were all hilariously cute covered in paint, eyes wide with excitement.

For my next job, she wanted me to cover an upcoming fundraiser by one of the East End Beach Mardi Gras krewes. They were a good group of folks who held an arts and crafts festival each spring to raise money for local charities. They needed help getting the word out to arts and crafts vendors that it was time to sign up. Naturally, I thought of Julian and wondered if he might want to get involved.

Summer had developed a peculiar interest in my work at the paper and asked if she could tag along and see what I did. I couldn't come up with a single reason to say no, so I took her with me that afternoon. She'd toned down the insults and seemed genuinely interested, so I was happy to discuss my small assignments with her and introduce her to Nancy. She hinted that she might be interested in a job, but I had no idea of her qualifications.

"I like taking pictures, and I've been playing around with layout software at home," Summer said. "Maybe I could be a photographer or help with paste-up."

"Maybe," I said, scrolling through the paper's inbox. "You could talk to Nancy about it, but they don't really have a big budget."

"So you were really involved in the bicentennial insert, right?"

It was odd that she was suddenly so nice and into me, but I chalked it up to her interest in a job. "I didn't write anything for it," I said. "But I helped find articles and pictures from the archives. Stuff like that."

"You worked on that piece about Mr. Kyser and Julian's mom, didn't you?"

"A little." *Where was she going with this?*

"You know I have a cousin who lives on Hammond Island. Not too far from the Kysers. Maybe you met her? Casey Simpson?"

My jaw almost hit the floor. "Casey Simpson's your cousin?"

"Uh-huh," she said, thoughtfully. "I think she dated Jack some before she left for Vandy."

I was stunned. Casey Simpson was the girl who had supposedly broken Jack's heart—right before he asked me out. I hadn't thought about her in six months.

"I never really met her, but I saw her once." I remembered her kissing Jack at the birthday party, and me running from the house. Julian had found me and comforted me. That warm memory of him carrying me back to his car, wanting us to take off and forget the Kysers, caused my lips to tighten.

"She's really pretty, don't you think?" Summer continued.

I nodded. "Very pretty. Do you talk to her much?" I wondered if Casey still kept up with Jack.

"Only when she's home."

"Oh." I didn't want to talk about it anymore. Jack was ancient history, and whether he kept up with his ex-girlfriend or not, didn't really concern me. I was getting more serious with Julian, and that was all I cared about now.

When I got home, I had the place to myself. I dug out the mail from our box and walked slowly inside doing my best not to think about Jack and Casey Simpson and Julian and me. I dropped the stack on the table and noticed a fat envelope in the mix with my name on it. The return address said Loyola University.

With trembling fingers, I picked it up and tore off the top. Inside was a long letter congratulating me on receiving their Scholarship for Academic Excellence and telling me all the great things it included. My breath rushed out in a *whoosh*—I'd done it! But for some reason, my excitement melted into really heavy sadness. I didn't want to look at the papers, and all at once, I felt very tired. I collected the contents and carried them up to my room. I stayed there through dinner, telling Mom I had homework and a headache.

My eyes were just closing when the telephone rang. It was Julian with our nightly check-in, and he was very upbeat. His afternoon with Blake had turned out as I'd hoped—blowtorch therapy. I smiled, thinking of his handsome face, and the sadness intensified in my stomach.

"I'm sorry I didn't see you much today," he said. "You sound tired."

"I am," I said, not wanting to tell him my big news. I couldn't explain why, but I didn't want to tell anyone. I didn't want it to be real yet. "Summer came with me to the paper office this afternoon," I said instead.

I could hear him frown. "Why'd you agree to that?"

"I don't know. She was interested, and… maybe I was too hard on her? She can't help it if her social skills need work."

"That's very mature." Then he laughed. "Did all that maturity wear you out?"

"Yes."

He laughed again. "Speaking of maturity, I'm feeling much better."

My forehead creased. "I'm glad, but what does that have to do with maturity?"

"I was thinking about our relationship rating," he said, then his voice lowered. "As in, my tree-climbing skills might've improved."

My heart ticked up in spite of my weird college-scholarship depression. "I'll unlock my window."

He breathed a smile in my ear, and I closed my eyes feeling much better. "Hey," he said. "I'm sorry about Friday."

My voice was equally quiet. "You don't have to apologize."

His voice was a low vibration that set my insides humming. "I was a little drunk, and you make me crazy."

A laugh escaped my lips. "I guess that's good?"

"So what are you wearing tonight?" He went on. "That little sleep shirt again? I'm thinking teeth this time."

"Teeth?" my forehead lined.

"I'm pulling it up with my teeth. Then I take my tongue…"

"I thought you were coming over," I said.

"I want to," he exhaled. "But Mom still hasn't left. We might have to wait one more night."

That news made me ridiculously sad again. Maybe I was getting my period. "You shouldn't tease me like that."

"You're the tease."

We said our goodbyes, and I was smiling as I hung up the phone, rolling onto my back under the covers. Snuggling under thicker blankets helped with missing him, but I wished Julian was wrapped up beside me now so much. I turned off the lights and settled in to sleep.

Sometime later I awoke. It was dark and my limbs were heavy with sleep, but someone was with me. I felt the warmth of his body on top of me, his hands rested lightly on each side of my face as he kissed me again and again. I kissed him back and tried to put my arms around him, but they were pinned against the bed. My body was filled with desire, and I felt the heat of his skin on my stomach, my arms, my inner thighs.

How had he gotten in? Did he climb the tree? I didn't know the answer. All I knew was I was powerless against his kisses, and waves of delight were pulsing me higher and higher with each movement of his body against mine. I heard a noise come from my throat, and his mouth moved to my neck. I opened my eyes and he lifted his head. Clear blue eyes looked into mine, but it wasn't who I thought. *It was Jack!*

I sat straight up in the bed with a gasp, but I was alone. No one was here. I panted as I looked around the dark room. My window was closed. It had all been a dream. I lay down again and pulled my knees into my chest. I was trembling, and I could still feel his kisses on my mouth. I lay motionless for several minutes replaying the scene in my mind. What was *that* about?

My biggest fear had been treating Julian like a rebound guy. Was my brain trying to tell me that was exactly what I was doing? Everything I believed felt shaken. It was like I'd been betrayed by my own body when I was completely unconscious and powerless. I fell asleep again troubled.

On Friday, it was announced at fourth period that Rachel and Brad had been voted Mardi Gras king and queen. Rachel was ecstatic, and I figured Brad was probably indifferent. He didn't care for that type of recognition, but he went along with anything that made Rachel happy.

Julian picked me up for the basketball game before the dance, and I smiled when I saw him sporting navy and white. "Who's got school spirit now?"

"I'm coming around," he smiled. "I just wasn't into it last week."

"I know." I went over and put my arms around his waist. "Still hurt?"

"Less and less." He leaned down and kissed my lips, and I felt a little thrill.

I'd decided to put my stupid dream behind me. For starters, dreams didn't mean anything—or if they did, they meant the opposite of what you thought. And second, I'd decided it was a combination of Mom's lasagna, shock from my scholarship acceptance letter (which was still in my bedroom under my bed), and worry about being separated from Julian.

"Did they announce the winners?" Mom asked, walking into the room.

"Rachel and Brad," I said, my arms still around his waist.

"I think you and Julian should've won it. Especially after Julian took one for the team."

I shook my head. "Seriously? No way."

"What? You're good-looking kids." I shook my head again, and she continued, assessing our outfits. "So you're skipping the ball?"

"I want to take Anna out instead," Julian said. "We might be a little late."

Mom smiled. "Okay, and have fun. Don't get into trouble."

"Yes, ma'am." Julian saluted. I giggled, pulling him out the door.

We arrived at the gym in time for the tip-off. Julian and I walked through the stands chatting with friends. I'd forgotten Rachel said alumni had been invited to the game, and the bleachers were jammed. We stopped off for drinks, and Julian lingered behind to talk to Blake. I spotted an empty row and was carefully making my way through the bodies when I noticed someone in my peripheral vision blocking my path.

I reached out to tap the person and a warm hand wrapped around mine. I looked up and almost dropped my drink.

"Oh, shit!" My hand clutched the paper cup so hard it collapsed.

"Hey, careful." He smiled and stepped closer to help me.

"Jack..."

The crowd was bustling around us, and with his body pushed close to me, I caught his familiar scent. It stole my breath.

"What are you doing here?" I managed to say, but I couldn't look at him. My stupid eyes had grown hot for some reason. It was like my whole body was betraying me. Again!

"Dad wanted me to come home for a visit." His voice had that low vibration I remembered. As always, my insides tried to go weak at the sound, and I clenched my jaw, fighting it. "Lucy wanted to come to the game."

"Lucy's here?" I looked quickly around the stands, trying to distract myself from the warmth of his hand still holding mine.

"Somewhere." I heard him smile, and my eyes blinked up to his. Then I blinked again. It was like I was looking into the sun. "How are you?" he said.

"Oh... I'm... good." I cleared my throat. This was ridiculous. I had to get a grip. "How are you?" I said in a firmer voice.

He shrugged. "Good, I guess."

Then I remembered Will telling their father he was skipping classes, drinking too much. "Really?" I really looked at him then.

"Sure," he said, meeting my gaze a little too intensely.

We were quiet, and he was too close. He hadn't changed a bit, and dammit I still cared. All I could think of was him in trouble, him alone, my dream. My dream that didn't mean what it seemed to mean. Just then Julian came up behind me.

"Jack." His voice snapped me out of my thoughts. "Hey, man." Julian reached around me to shake hands then put his hand on my waist.

135

"Julian." Jack released my hand, his eyes going to where Julian's rested. "Are you two dating now?"

"Oh… uh…" I looked down.

"Yep," Julian answered.

Jack nodded, pressing his lips together. I remembered that look from the hay maze last fall. It was how he'd looked right after he'd realized Julian had kissed me. That I had kissed Julian back.

"I'm taking off," he said. "It was nice seeing you again, Anna."

He left, and I felt like the wind had been knocked out of me.

"You okay?" Julian asked.

I looked at him and smiled weakly. "I think so."

As always, he put his arm over my shoulder. "That was unexpected."

I nodded, not sure how to proceed. "It really was."

He studied my face a beat, then he lowered his arm, catching my hand. "Still want to stay here or you ready to go?"

"I don't know." I blinked up at those blue eyes, almost identical to his brother's. "Maybe we should go?"

He nodded, and we left the stands. We walked back toward the car, and I slid my hand through Julian's arm. Hugging myself close to his side, I leaned my head on his shoulder. "Where we headed?"

"I don't know. I was thinking we could get something to eat if you're hungry or go down to the pier or take a walk. Just spend some time together. It hasn't been just us in weeks."

"I've got to be honest with you. I'm feeling so tired right now." It was stupid, but I felt like I'd run a marathon. And I wasn't sure if I'd won it.

He held the door, studying my face. "Want to go home?"

"Would you be upset?"

Julian shook his head. "Home it is."

We drove back to my house, and Mom was still up. "You guys are early! What happened?"

"Oh, nothing. I just... I've just been so tired lately." Ever since my college papers arrived, although I wasn't sure why. And then tonight, seeing Jack. It all felt like way too much hitting me all at once, and I just wanted to hide for a while and process it all.

"Are you catching something?" Mom walked over and put her hand on my forehead.

"Don't think so." I said.

She glanced from me to Julian then she tossed the remote on the couch. "I was just going to my room. You guys make yourselves comfortable. Order a movie."

Julian and I sat on the couch facing each other. We laced our fingers, and he pulled my hand to his lips. "Is this about Jack?"

My stomach squirmed, but I wouldn't lie to him. "A little."

His lips pressed together. "Do you want me to stay?"

I nodded feeling my eyes grow damp. I slid forward and put my arms around his middle. He held me close and stroked the back of my hair. We stayed that way for several minutes. Finally, he moved me back on the couch and stood. "Go to bed. I'll be back later."

My eyes went to his ribs. "Aren't you still—"

He smiled and went to the door. "It'll be okay."

I watched him leave and then went upstairs. After washing my face, I walked across the hall to my room, unlocking the window before sliding under the covers.

I'd planned to read for a while, but instead I turned off the light and fell asleep.

This time when I awoke, I knew I wasn't dreaming. Julian was sliding in with me. He pulled me close to him as he covered my mouth with his, and I held onto him tightly, his hand rubbing my back. His lips moved to my cheek and then my temple.

"I'm so glad you're here." I whispered.

"Mm-hm." He continued kissing behind my ear, down to my neck as he rolled me over and pulled my back into his chest.

"Did it hurt getting in?" I asked.

"Not so much." His fingers were stroking the length of my arm. I laced mine with his.

"I'm sorry I didn't feel like doing anything tonight." I said.

His lips pressed to the top of my shoulder, sending that wonderful tingle down my body. "It's okay," he whispered. "You had a shock."

Guilt pushed the happy tingles away, and I chewed my lip. "I'm sorry I was shocked," I whispered.

"You couldn't help it."

I rolled forward and turned to face him. "Are you mad at me?"

My eyes had grown used to the dark, and I could see him smile. "Am I acting mad?"

"No," I shook my head, studying his mouth. "But I mean, you must be thinking something."

He reached forward and pulled me into a hug, my cheek resting on his chest. "I'm thinking you saw your old boyfriend, and it rattled you. It happens. Should I be thinking anything else?"

I exhaled, hugging his waist. "I guess not."

His lips were at my ear. "I can't pretend he never existed. I had to watch you follow him around like a puppy all last fall. It was pretty sick. But that's over, right?"

I nodded. "I think so."

He pulled back then. "You think so?"

My body felt hot and cold at once, and I wanted to throw up. But I had to tell him the truth. I'd always been honest with Julian... unlike some people. "It's only been a few months since it hurt bad, but for the last several weeks, I haven't thought of him at all." Other than my stupid dream.

Julian propped his head on his hand. "And how do you feel now?"

I thought for a second. "I feel like I'm *so* glad you're here."

He smiled and traced my lips with his finger. "Why?"

I smiled, reaching up and threading those fingers with mine. "Because you always make me feel better."

He leaned forward and kissed my nose. "Why?" he whispered.

I shrugged. "I don't know... you just do somehow. That's all."

He shook his head and chuckled.

I frowned. "What?"

He lowered his head and pulled my back into his chest again.

"What?" I repeated softly, wrapping his strong arms around me.

"Forget it. What's the latest on college? Any news?"

My lips pressed together, and my bottom lip went between my teeth. I had to tell him. He needed to know. But we'd just made it through my last confession. I'd reacted badly to seeing Jack, and I couldn't forget his annoyance last Friday about Loyola and Tulane being steps apart.

"I'm still waiting to hear from everyone," I hedged.

Closing my eyes, I knew I couldn't keep this a secret much longer. Rachel was waiting to hear as well. Apartment complexes had to have deposits and references.

"Well, I know how excited I was about getting into Savannah." He was stroking my arm again. "I hope you get what you want."

My forehead lined. "Even if it means I go to Loyola?"

"Sure," he kissed my ear. "If you go to Loyola, we'll figure out what happens next."

I turned over and put my arms around him and snuggled into his chest. I wasn't sure I could sleep. I was frustrated with myself for not telling him everything. But I had time, and tonight, I just wanted to hold him and feel his arms around me. I took a deep breath, inhaling his fresh, beachy scent I loved.

"Can we just sleep now?" I whispered against his skin.

For a moment he didn't speak. Then he gave me a squeeze, kissing the top of my head. "Sure."

Chapter 14

Spring break was approaching, and after that, we'd be racing toward the finish line with only prom standing between us and graduation. It made me sick and nervous and happy at the same time. I hated the end was looming before us, but I couldn't deny I was excited about college and the future. My only heaviness came when I tried to fit me and Julian into the picture.

Julian was welding again and busy turning the sketches he'd made for the last several weeks into three-dimensional works of art. I still hadn't figured out a way to tell him about Loyola. I needed to do it, but I was afraid he'd ask me how long I'd known. Then I was worried he'd be angry that I hadn't told him right away. I knew the longer I waited the worse it got, but he'd gone from mentioning it all the time to never mentioning it at all. And it was hard to work into conversations.

I'd texted Rachel with the news, and I hoped she and I could talk about apartments and stuff at lunch. It was my plan for letting him know—he could hear us talking, and I'd tell him I'd just found out. But Rachel was tied up planning a senior bonfire and hadn't been around during lunch all week.

After school, I had to stop by the paper office, and Julian suggested I drop by the garage and watch him work when I was done. I agreed and had my camera ready to take pictures of him working. I also made a firm resolution that this would be the day I'd tell him about Loyola. Of course, I also had to tell my parents. Suddenly college and the future and separation all felt very real, and that sadness pushed even harder in my chest. I didn't want to think about what was going to happen to us. I just wanted to be happy with Julian, being his girlfriend.

I arrived at the garage a little after five, and I could hear him inside. He'd been collecting pieces of fencing and other large items of scrap to assemble the bench scene he'd shown me. I stopped and put my jacket back in the car. It was still cool, but not enough to compete with the heat generated by the blowtorch in his small garage. Then I remembered how he pulled off his shirt sometimes when he worked and smiled, hoping it would be one of those days. I didn't expect to hear a girl's voice as I got closer.

Peeking around the door, I nearly lost it when I saw Renee sitting on his worktable. Her shiny brown hair hung loose down her back, and she was wearing a low-cut blouse and short skirt. Her legs were uncrossed. I could read that body language a mile away, and I was furious. Julian didn't seem to notice as he moved several of the large pieces of fencing he'd collected to the back of the garage.

"So you're finally dating Anna Sanders," Renee said, dropping her head to the side and swinging one of her knees together. "Jesus, Julian, what was that? Some personal goal of yours?"

I really hated Renee.

Julian paused, and it was like he suddenly saw her, slutting it up on his worktable. "What are you up to?" he said.

"Nothing," she laughed and actually tried to play innocent. "She's just such a nun. And she never took you seriously."

He hefted up another piece of fencing. "You never took me seriously."

"How could I?" she cried. "You were always so distracted. I could never hold your attention for more than five minutes."

He walked back, rubbing his palms together. "I lasted more than five minutes."

"Mmm... That's what I was thinking about today." She reached out and caught his arm, and her voice turned into a purr. "It's been a while since we were together."

He didn't pull away like I wished he would, and for a moment, I almost ran in and started yelling. But I had to know how this would play out between them.

Julian frowned. "Aren't you dating some guy at Fulton?"

Renee slid her hand down his arm and lifted his hand into her lap. "Keeping up with me? I like that."

"I just heard Rachel talking to Brad," he said, pulling his hand away. "But I'm where I want to be, so it's cool."

"I don't believe it." Renee pushed her hair back and leaned forward, showing cleavage. "We were so hot together."

He shook his head. "Don't do that."

He stepped around her, picking up one of the sketches and then going to his pile of scrap. Renee hopped down and followed him.

"Rachel said they'd be living together at Loyola next year," she said. "That must sting knowing how close she'll be to Jack."

My breath caught as my eyes went wide. I didn't think it was possible to hate Renee any more than I did at that very moment.

But when I heard Julian's tone, my hate turned to panic. "What's that?" he frowned.

"She didn't tell you? Anna the Nerd got some major, full-ride scholarship. Rachel said they've been apartment hunting for weeks."

"No." Julian had stopped working and leaned against the table beside her. I saw the side of his jaw clench, and I desperately wanted to run in and explain. But I was frozen in place. "I knew she was waiting on her best offer."

"Well, lucky Anna." Renee reached over and ran a finger down the side of Julian's arm. He glanced at her, and she stepped forward to catch his chin. "I'm not going anywhere." I closed my eyes as she kissed him and rolled my back against the wall. I could feel the tears in my throat. He would never understand, and it served me right if I lost him to that super-ho Renee.

"You'd better take off," I heard him say, and I crept back in case she was leaving in this direction. When I got outside, I leaned against my car. What could I tell him now? I had to get in there. I had to explain. I pulled myself together and strode toward the garage as Renee was coming out.

"Hey, Anna," she smirked looking me up and down.

"Hey yourself," I spat back.

Inside, Julian was still leaning against the table. He was looking down as if he was trying to decide what to do next. I went over to him and slid my arms around his waist. Maybe if I acted like I didn't know what just happened, I could smooth things over by just telling him. Like I'd meant to all along.

"Hey," I said, kissing his cheek.

He reached for my arms and pushed me back to face him. Pain shot through the sides of my stomach when I saw his expression. "Renee just left."

"I saw her," I tried to stay light. "And I'm completely ticked. Is she trying to steal my guy?"

"She said something about Rachel and you being roommates at Loyola next year." His blue eyes held mine. So much for acting innocent.

"I guess Rachel told her," I said quietly. "But we've been talking about living together for a while. We only just finalized everything."

"When were you *finally* going to tell me?" He was clearly mad, and I didn't know what to say to fix it.

"I was going to tell you..." But I wasn't really sure why I'd kept the news to myself. "It's a great scholarship, and I think it's the best offer I'm going to get."

He nodded. "So you're going to Loyola next year."

I reached for him again, but he stopped me. "Julian, please..."

"Maybe you should go home," he exhaled, stepping past me. "I'm not really up for this anymore."

I followed him quickly, pain radiating through my chest. "Up for what? What are you thinking? This doesn't change anything between us."

He turned back then. "It doesn't? No, you're right. It doesn't change anything for you, but it changes things for me."

I shook my head, trying not to cry. "I don't understand. Why?"

"It's like all this time we've been together, you've just been passing time. Waiting to decide."

"Decide what? I already decided. I want to be with you!"

"Then why didn't you tell me about this? Why do you always hold back?"

145

"I don't know. I just..." I shook my head. "I don't know how to explain it. I was afraid, and things are changing..." The miserable truth that had held me silent for days finally appeared clearly in my head. "What if we don't stay together next year?"

"I want us to be together next year," he said. "But maybe you want to keep your options open."

"I don't! I only applied to schools in New Orleans because Jack and I were still together then. But everything's different now. Now there's us."

He leaned back against the worktable again, studying the floor. "You should've told me."

"I know." I quickly closed the space between us. "I'm sorry. I just didn't want you to get the wrong idea. I didn't want you to be mad, and... I wasn't sure how I felt about it."

I studied his eyes, still focused elsewhere, still thinking something I couldn't tell. All the heaviness of the past several days, all my fears, were pushing so hard inside me. I felt like I'd explode, and I wanted to kiss him so badly. I wanted him to kiss me, to take this pain away. I slid my arms around his waist, and this time he didn't stop me as I lifted my lips to his. He kissed me, but it wasn't right. He didn't pull me to him, and when I stepped back, I knew he was still upset.

"It won't work," he said, shaking his head. "I can't be in Savannah and you in New Orleans with him. Especially with you not telling me stuff. I don't want us to end that way."

Pain hit me like a medicine ball right in the guts. "No, Julian. Don't do this."

He shook his head. "It's easier to do it now."

"It is not easier!" My voice was loud, and I grabbed both his arms.

"I think we should go back to being just friends," he said, straightening up and pushing my hands away.

I stepped back as my breath caught in my throat. The tears were flooding my eyes, on the brink of spilling over. I turned to run out. I wouldn't cry in front of him. My heart was smashing into a million pieces, and all I could think was how far we'd come, everything we'd said, the nights we'd spent together. How could he just quit on us?

I made it to the car and climbed inside. I could barely see to drive, but I had to get out of here. Pulling onto the road, I gasped a painful breath as the first tears hit my cheeks. This was my fault. What was wrong with me? Why didn't I tell him? Everything I'd lost slammed into my mind over and over with each passing minute — Julian's clear blue eyes and his soft laugh, him slipping into my bed and holding me all night. I looked down at the dragonfly ring sparkling on my finger, and sobs shook my body violently. Oh, God. This couldn't be happening.

Chapter 15

Breaking up with Julian was so much worse than breaking up with Jack. At least Jack had broken up with me early, and even though he kept coming around confusing the situation, I wasn't constantly bombarded with months of happy memories. And I never saw him at school.

Math loomed in front of me like a horrible nightmare. I took a different route to class, walking as slowly as I could, but as I approached the door, I froze. Where was Mrs. Harris? She was always standing there scowling. Did she have a sub? If she did, I was cutting class.

I stood at the door and tried to decide what to do.

"Going in?" My whole body tensed at the sound of Julian's voice.

I looked down and clutched my books closer to my chest. He breathed an annoyed sigh and jerked the door open. I watched his tall, slender body move ahead of me to his seat. My chair, the one right beside his, was empty, so I quickly sat down at the first desk to my right in the very back row. Montage came bustling in and froze.

"Aw, no, Anna," he said as he towered over me.

I realized I'd taken his seat, but I gave him pleading eyes. He glanced at my empty chair in the front beside Julian.

"I'm not sittin up there," he said. Then he grabbed the skinny guy in the desk in front of me and pushed him down the aisle. "You just got promoted, Poindexter."

Montage threw his books on the ejected student's desk and sat down. The boy straightened his clothes and slouched into my former seat. Julian glanced up at him, then looked back at me and shook his head.

At lunch, I relocated back inside the cafeteria to the senior table, and I had the pleasure of sharing my cold sandwich with Summer.

"What's going on? Aren't you always with Julian?" she asked in her typically insensitive manner.

"We're taking a break." I said quietly.

"A break!" she cried. "Is it because of Renee Barron?"

I glared at her. "No."

"I don't understand relationships," she shook her head. "You two seemed pretty happy."

"We were," I mumbled, picking at my sandwich.

"So who dumped who?"

My eyes cut to her, and she was lucky I was too miserable to sock her. "Can we talk about something else?"

"Sure!" she smiled. "Mind if I go to the paper office with you again? I really liked Nancy."

I shrugged. "Meet me after school, and we can ride together."

I couldn't believe I was low enough to be spending time with stupid Summer. And now I'd agreed to take her to the paper office, the one place that was mine. Hopefully, Nancy would send me off on an assignment, and I could ditch her there.

My sandwich tasted like a sponge, and I stuffed it back in the bag when I looked up and saw Julian enter the cafeteria. I quickly leaned forward, putting my hand on my forehead. He walked to the other end of the senior table and sat down by Scotty. I wasn't sure what he was doing, so I finished with Summer and quickly collected my things and left. Rachel was in our old spot waving me over. It was the first time I'd seen her all week.

She tossed her blonde hair back. "I'm away party planning and everything falls to pieces," she said. "What's going on?"

"I don't know what you mean." My voice sounded dead.

"Julian's in a mood. He just got up and left," she said. "Are you two fighting?"

I shook my head. "We broke up."

"What the hell?" she cried. "Was it Renee?"

"Oh my God! Why does everybody keep saying that?"

Rachel shrugged. "She seems to pop up wherever he is. I couldn't think of any other reason. You two were pretty hot and heavy."

Those words made me want to roll into the fetal position. "It's not Renee," I said in a quieter voice.

"Then what in the world happened? I was sure you were in it for the long haul."

Her words made my throat hurt. "I gotta go." I whispered and hurried away.

I didn't start crying then, but at the end of the day when I saw Summer waiting by my car I nearly did. I couldn't do this.

"Hey, Summer," I said. "I don't feel like work today. I'm going to call in sick."

Her lips pressed into a disapproving smirk. "You shouldn't let your professional life suffer when your personal life goes bad."

My eyes pressed closed, and I did not curse at her. "Thanks. I'll remember that when I have a real job."

Her brow lined. "You don't get paid at the paper?"

"Yes, I get paid."

"Then it sounds like a real job to me."

I wondered if I could get away with accidentally hitting Summer with my car. "You're right," I said. "I should be more responsible. Let's go."

We arrived at the office in Fairview, and Nancy was nice enough to remember Summer from her last visit. "I liked those pictures you sent over," she said. "I could give you some freelance jobs if you're interested."

"Sure!" Summer was practically bouncing. "Whatcha got?"

"Come in my office, and I'll show you."

I couldn't believe Nancy was giving Summer a job. I couldn't believe I'd contaminated my workplace like this.

"Oh, Anna?" Nancy called back. "Bill Kyser called for you. He said he'd be around this week if you wanted to return that paper? Do you know what he's talking about?"

"Yeah," I nodded, dropping into the chair at the little makeshift desk we'd put together at the beginning of last semester. "Thanks. I'll take care of it."

The old computer was still covered in yellowing papers, and mail was piling up around it. I grabbed a letter opener and started slicing the top off the envelopes. I hadn't been keeping up with all the press releases, but I decided now was as good a time as any to bury myself in them.

I was halfway through tossing items more than two weeks old when Summer returned. "Thanks for letting me come with you," she said.

"Sure," I said, checking dates.

"It's going to be fun working together," she continued. "Don't you think?"

I nodded not looking up.

"So Nancy said you got a call from Bill Kyser. That's Jack's dad, isn't it?"

"Um-hm," I said.

"Was it something with Jack?"

"What?" I finally looked up at her. She was watching me curiously. "No. It's nothing. Just a paper he gave me when I was helping Nancy with the bicentennial insert. He needs me to return it."

"Anything newsworthy?" she pressed. "Want me to go with you and take a picture of you giving it back?"

I almost laughed out loud at the thought. "No. It's nothing."

"Bill Kyser, the richest, most powerful man in East End Beach calls you, and you say it's nothing?" Her eyes were huge.

"Jeez, Summer. You make it sound like the president called." I slammed the press releases down and stood. "Our job is to talk to people who make things happen in the community. They're going to call us back. That's how it works."

"But you said you didn't do any writing on the bicentennial insert. How does that work?"

I looked at her for a second. Why was she pressing so hard on this? I knew Summer's personality was obnoxious, but this seemed too much. Even for her.

Suddenly, I had an idea. "The truth is," I lowered my voice as if I were telling her a big secret, "he loaned me this book about East End Beach. I think it was a very expensive first edition, and I lost it. What should I do?"

She leaned back as if she hadn't expected me to say that. "Tell him?"

"But like you just said, he's so rich and powerful," I continued, trying to sound really anxious. "What if he gets mad at me?"

"Want me to help you look for it?" She stood. "Maybe it's under all this junk…"

"No." I shook my head. "I looked there already."

"Does Nancy know?" She continued lifting stacks of papers, and I watched her little wild goose chase a moment.

"No, and please don't tell her," I said. "Please don't tell *anyone*."

"Okay," she said with a shrug. "Then I guess I'd better get going."

I watched her go with suspicion, wondering what she was up to. If she were spying on me for some reason, that fake book routine would expose her. I just had to wait and see who showed up saying they knew I was looking for an expensive first edition belonging to Mr. Kyser.

My moment of intrigue got me through the rest of the day, but when I finally made it back to my house, all my former emotions hit me strong as ever. I walked into my bedroom, and the first thing I saw was my window. I strode over to it and turned the lock. If it was over, there was no use having my bedroom window unlocked.

Then I turned to my desk and pulled out the Loyola envelope. Mom and Dad had been so proud and excited when I'd finally shown it to them. I took out the letter and read it again. My tuition would be paid in full as long as I maintained my grade point average. I also had a campus job if I wanted it. I'd forgotten to ask Nancy about the status of me working at the New Orleans paper, but I'd talk to her about it tomorrow. I started reading about college, and soon my eyes were filling. I crawled under my quilt and refused to let myself cry.

Chapter 16

The next day, I adopted a determined stride as I approached our shared class. I walked right through the door, past my teacher's raised eyebrows, but when I reached Montage's old desk, I froze. Julian was leaning back in the chair. Montage was sitting at the desk in front of it, and the two were laughing.

Julian looked up at me. "Can I help you?" he said.

My jaw dropped as my stomach twisted into painful knots. I couldn't believe he could sit there acting happy. Without a word, I turned and went to his old seat and put my books down. The relocated kid was in my former chair. I opened my textbook and started reading the explanation of formulas I'd barely noticed a week ago. It felt like a pill was stuck in my throat, but after that entrance, after him actually being able to *laugh*, I'd be damned if I let Julian see how miserable I was.

I knew from experience that if I held on, the pain I felt practically every minute of every day would gradually begin to fade. Over the break, I'd had Julian to distract me from losing Jack. I didn't have anyone to distract me from losing Julian. That made me worry it might take longer, until I got to lunch and saw Summer happily waiting for me at the senior table.

"Hi, Anna!" she chirped. "I had a great idea for finding that book."

My forehead wrinkled. "What?" Then I remembered my ruse yesterday.

"You could call Jack and tell him! I bet he'd help you figure out the title, and then you could replace it."

I shook my head, sitting down. "I'm not calling Jack."

"But you're friends, right?" Her voice was starting to feel like a rash on my skin. Irritating. "I saw you talking to him at the game. I bet he'd be glad to help you."

My eyes flashed to hers. "Why were you following me at the game?"

She laughed. "I wasn't following you. I just saw you there, and I saw you talking to Jack."

I shook my head, evaluating my repeat, cold-sandwich lunch. "We just bumped into each other."

"Is that what happened with Julian?" She went on, stirring the contents of her thermos. "He got mad because you were talking to Jack?"

I dropped the sandwich then. "Listen, Summer. You're going to have to stop being such a pushy pain in the ass if we're going to be friends, got it?"

She actually looked surprised by my words. "I don't understand."

"Stop telling me what you think I ought to do, and stop meddling in my private life."

She stopped eating and was quiet. For a moment I felt bad. I almost apologized, knowing my delivery had been extra harsh because of how I was feeling about Julian, but unexpectedly she brightened up. "Okay," she said and went back to eating.

I just stared at her. I couldn't figure Summer out, and then I had the strangest thought. Maybe I'd been making things harder than they needed to be with her. We finished lunch, and I collected my things. The bell was ringing, and she happily packed up, telling me bye before heading to class.

I walked away completely puzzled. I was frowning when I opened the door and nearly ran right into Julian. *Jesus!*

"Oh, sorry," he said, hands in his pockets. I studied them, wondering if he ever looked at his little dragonfly tattoo. If when he saw it he thought of me and missed me as badly as I missed him. "You're eating lunch with Summer now?" he said.

I nodded, not looking up. "So?"

"So I don't have to hang out in the quad." The softness in his voice made my chest ache. *Why was he doing this?* "I don't mind sitting with Scotty or Blake during lunch. I know Summer makes you crazy."

"Thanks." I whispered. Those pains were back, shooting through my stomach. I had to get out of here before I lost it. "She's not so bad."

I hurried to my next class without looking behind me.

I didn't have any more run-ins with Julian after that, and even Summer toned down her game of twenty questions. I chided myself for not saying something to her sooner once I realized how easy it was to get her off my case.

By Friday, I'd decided to join Rachel with Brad in the quad. As promised, Julian was nowhere to be seen.

"Hey! I've missed you, roomie!" Rachel said with a smile. "'bout time you rejoined the group."

"Thanks."

"How's it going?"

"Okay, I guess." I looked down. Brad glanced over at me and then back to Rachel.

She smiled. "Can I do anything?"

"Yeah," I said, feeling a strange surge of empowerment. "Tell me about this bonfire you've been planning all semester. What's the deal?"

She perked up at that. "It's going to be *so* great. It's just for the seniors, but you can bring a date... or not." She gave me a worried look, as if she expected me to instantly break down sobbing.

"Can I bring a friend?" I said quickly, wanting her to resume talking.

"Of course! And your date — or friend — can be any grade."

I nodded. "I think it's a neat tradition you're starting."

She suddenly seemed excited again. "So are you coming?"

"Sure." I studied my sandwich, still not hungry. "And it's tomorrow night?"

"Yep! First Saturday of spring break."

"Good. And it's still cool enough for a bonfire," I said, putting my lunch back in my bag. I wondered when I'd feel like eating again.

"Great for snuggling." She grinned leaning back against Brad. I smiled and looked down. "Oh, sorry." She straightened up again.

"No! It is. You're right. It's great weather for snuggling." My throat ached, and I wanted to cry saying the words. "See ya there."

I decided to stick to the cafeteria in the future. It was great seeing my old friends, but sitting there with them reminded me too much of Julian. And watching Brad and Rachel be affectionate with each other was like a kick in the stomach that left me weak and winded. I walked inside and made my way to where Summer was sitting.

She glanced up as I approached, and I could tell she was ready to launch the cross-examination. "I thought you were eating with Rachel today?"

"I was," I said, sitting beside my new... friend? "She mentioned the bonfire tomorrow. You going?"

"Probably not." She looked down, stirring the contents of her ever-present thermos. "I don't have a date."

"Me either. But it sounds like fun. Want to ride over together?"

Her eyes blinked mine. "Really?"

"Sure, why not?"

"I'll be at your house at seven!"

The bell rang, and the mood on campus shifted in a palpable way. It was as if everyone realized at the same time we were only a few hours away from the last break of the year, and a distinct giddiness swept over the campus. The only problem was my broken heart was impervious to it.

I watched my fellow classmates beaming at each other and acting like they were hopped up on moon pies and felt distinctly like the odd ball. It was as if I'd been transported to another world where the inhabitants were all happy, smiling sunbeams, and I was a little black cloud. I hugged my books closer to my chest and walked to my locker, wondering if anyone would notice if I left. I removed the books I needed to study for exams, closed my locker, and walked to my car. I'd never cut school in my life, but I got in the car, cranked the engine, and drove home.

The house was empty when I got there, and it was cold because the heater had been turned off. I didn't bother to turn it on. I simply dropped my books on the counter and walked up the stairs. I lowered the shades in my room, pulled off my boots, and climbed under the blankets. In a few minutes, I was asleep.

Chapter 17

When I opened my eyes again it was the next day. I was still wearing my school clothes, and I'd slept all night. Alone. I fought against the sadness that tried to rush over me like a wave. Mom was downstairs making coffee, so I went down and sat at the bar.

She looked up and poured me a cup. "Want to talk about it now?" she asked.

I didn't raise my head. "Julian broke up with me."

"Why?" she said, leaning forward on the bar, not sounding surprised enough.

"Because I didn't tell him about Loyola."

That surprised her. "I thought he knew about Loyola?"

"He knew I applied, but he didn't know I was definitely going."

She straightened up and crossed her arms. "Honey, that doesn't make any sense. If you applied, the chances were very good that you were definitely going."

"I know, right?" I looked up, thinking she was on my side, but she was still being neutral.

"What else happened?" she said.

I shrugged. "That's all. Renee went and told him, which *I* should've been mad about—she was practically all over him. But he turned it into something about Jack. Like I didn't tell him because I was keeping my options open or something."

Mom looked down for a second. "Were you?"

"No! I didn't tell anybody! But it wasn't because of Jack. I don't know what it was." My eyes were watery. "He didn't even try to understand."

She exhaled, and our arms were almost touching on the bar. "Julian's been at your side for months, Anna. He's a bright, attractive guy. You've got to make a decision."

"I did make a decision! I was with him! How else could we have broken up?"

She shook her head. "He must've sensed some hesitation. Did you say you were sorry?"

"Yes."

"Do you want to get back together?"

"Yes!" Even with him acting like he'd moved on, I missed him so bad it hurt. I felt like he'd reached in and pulled my heart out and walked off with it. I could barely look at my window or my ring or the dolphin in the quad or even wrought-iron fencing without tears. I'd started chewing spearmint gum I was so miserable.

She moved around and leaned beside me. "Did you tell him that?"

"No," I said softly.

"Why not?"

"I don't think it matters to him anymore," I said quietly.

"Or maybe that's all he needs to hear."

Tears were forming quickly. "He wants me to beg?" I sniffed. I could almost visualize me doing it.

"Not beg." Mom reached over and smoothed my hair back. "Just say clearly that you want to be with him."

I shook my head. It couldn't be that easy.

She patted my cheek gently. "Know what? Just give it some time. Julian really likes you. I bet he comes around."

I decided to wear old jeans and a sweater to the bonfire. My talk with Mom had only made me feel worse, and I almost called Summer to cancel. If it hadn't been senior year, I probably would've.

She arrived right at seven, and I drove us to the Hawkins farm. It was the same location as the Halloween hay maze, and the memories of kissing Julian in October were almost too much. Still, I pushed through. The faculty and several parents had erected a huge pile of logs, and they were just starting the blaze when we walked up. Slowly the flames grew, and after a few minutes, the night sky was brilliantly lit with orange and yellow, tiny sparks flickered up into the air like fireflies from the dry wood.

Some of the mothers were setting out supplies to make s'mores, and a few of our musical classmates had formed a circle to play guitars and sing. I walked through the crowd waving and doing my best to smile and socialize. I picked up a marshmallow, but I ended up tossing it in the fire. A chocolate square was more what I wanted. I leaned against the supply table eating the rich, sugary treat, watching my classmates enjoy themselves. The bonfire was warm on the cool night. If everything were different, it would've been the perfect event to share with Julian. I could just imagine sitting on one of the logs, his arms around me. I'd probably lean back and kiss his neck. A sniff jerked my chest, and I took another bite of chocolate. This was a bad idea.

Rachel and Brad finally showed up, and I walked over to greet them. "I think you've created a tradition, Rach," I said. "Everybody seems to love it."

"Thanks," she smiled, holding Brad's arm. "So who's your friend?"

"Oh, I just rode over with Summer Daigle. She's roasting marshmallows, I think."

"I didn't know you two hung out." Rachel looked like she was about to start laughing. "Isn't she a bit... much?"

"Yes!" I answered loudly.

Rachel burst out laughing then. "So what's the deal?"

I shrugged, pushing my hands into my front pockets and feeling the tiniest bit less miserable. "One day I finally lost it and told her to knock it off, and guess what?"

"What?"

"She did!"

We both laughed then, and it felt good to smile for a change. "I think you had a learning experience." Rachel said, but her expression instantly changed. "Don't look now," she exhaled quietly.

Her eyes traveled behind me, and I turned in time to see Julian walking up with Renee hanging on his arm. For a split second my knees gave out, and I thought I might fall. But I caught Rachel's arm and turned back to face her, doing my best to keep my expression neutral.

"Hey! Rachel and *Anna*!" Renee called out. Her smug grin twisted my insides, and she tried to dash over to us. But Julian hung back.

"Great bonfire," Renee said, joining us alone. "Why didn't we do this last year?"

"Because you didn't have a brilliant head cheerleader to come up with it last year," Rachel said. I hated that they were friends.

"Of course. I should've known," Renee smiled.

The two continued talking, and Julian slowly joined us. I couldn't look at his face, but I watched Renee's fingers tighten on his arm. It felt like they were tightening around my throat. When our eyes met briefly, his didn't seem happy. Or maybe that was what I wanted to see. I blinked away the mist clouding mine.

"I didn't think you'd be here," he said quietly.

I couldn't answer. It was like I was back on that other planet again, only my heart and stomach and insides had been left on Earth. I was hollow and miserable.

"You okay?" Rachel said to me.

I shook my head, trying to break the spell. "I think I'm going home."

My voice sounded strange, everything sounded strange. I made my way to my car feeling like I was alone in a tunnel, and I had to get to the end of it before I lost control. I didn't worry about Summer. She'd find a way home. There were plenty of parents here. I just had to leave. I had to crawl under my bed and never come out. I had to get as far away as I possibly could. Two weeks wasn't long enough to get over this. No amount of time would be.

At home, I opted for *in* my bed instead of under it. I lay in the silent room for many long minutes before crawling back out again and putting on soft music to fill the empty air with sound. Maybe it would help me sleep. Back under my blankets, I lay very still listening, thinking.

I was in love with him. No questions, no hesitation. Love. And it was too late. He was leaving for Savannah in a few months, I was headed to Loyola. He'd ended it, and on top of everything, now he was apparently back with Renee.

I wanted to throw up when I imagined her putting her hands on him. The very thought of him sleeping with her hurt so bad. Tears burned in my eyes, and my stomach clenched. I wanted to scream and cry and hit everything. I wanted to smash and break and tear things—starting with that scholarship letter.

But that wasn't right. I was really happy and proud of that scholarship. Getting a full ride to an expensive private school was a huge deal. I just hadn't meant for it to cost me Julian.

A huge teddy bear sat in the corner of my bedroom. It had been a twelfth birthday present, and it was nearly as big as me. I pulled him into the bed behind me and grabbed one of his huge paws, wrapping it around my waist as a hot tear slid down my nose. Stupid me. Stupid Julian. Stupid everything.

My shoulders shook as I wept. I knew he was a big part of my life, but I'd never realized just how big until now, lying here, missing him like crazy, feeling like I had lost the best thing that would ever happen to me in my entire life.

I slid my palm across the mattress, imagining it was his chest. I closed my eyes and saw the round tattoo he'd inked, remembering the day he'd stopped me in the parking lot to show it to me. He always showed me everything he did. I remembered the times he'd caught my curls and held them back to smile at me, and the feel of his fingers on mine as he measured them for my ring. I remembered sitting by his bed all night in the hospital, waiting for him to wake up after the car crash when we'd almost lost him. Lastly, and most painfully, I remembered his kiss.

A low, painful groan rose from deep in my stomach, and I sat up and threw the bear on the floor. Just then I heard a soft tap on my window. Our eyes met through the glass, and I was across the room and undoing the lock before my feet even touched the floor.

Julian slid through the opening and onto the rug with me as our lips found each others'. I could barely breathe. All I could do was hold his shoulders and kiss him again and again.

"Oh, Julian." I whispered, my cheeks wet with tears.

He smoothed my hair back from my face and looked into my eyes. I almost couldn't believe it. What was he doing here? His hands held my cheeks, and for a moment we simply blinked at each other. I slid my hands to his, and we both smiled. He lowered his face and kissed me again, soft and slow. His warm lips parted mine as our tongues lightly touched. Happiness bloomed in my chest, and I leaned forward to hug him. Just to press his warm body to mine. It was so good.

After a minute, I sat back. "But... Renee?"

He laced our fingers in his lap. "Left her at the bonfire. She can catch a ride with Rachel." He pulled my hand up to kiss it. "I couldn't stand seeing you so sad. I can't stand us being apart."

I pulled his face to mine again, kissing him as hard as I could. He moved me onto his lap, and I reached down, tugging on his sweater. He quickly whipped it off, and our lips reconnected as my hands slid down his bare back. His low groan thrilled me, and I hugged him even closer. It was so good to be in this place again, and I wanted so much more. I never wanted to let him go

His fingers slipped beneath my shirt, and when he touched my skin, I pulled away. We were both breathing fast, and his brow creased. "What?" he breathed.

It was time. I had to tell him everything. Well, not everything. His parents' secret had to stay between us, but otherwise, he needed to know everything.

I took a breath and blurted. "I've never done it before, and I'm a little nervous."

I paused and the room was silent. He still seemed confused, and my throat went dry, which made me talk even faster. "I mean, I am. And maybe a little intimidated. Because of Renee and all... And I'm sorry for that. But I know I love you. I really do. And I want to be with you, and I want *it* to be with you. I mean, I'm not saying no. I'm not saying anything. I don't know why I said that." I rubbed my forehead and kept going, trying to get it right. "I mean, now that I know how I feel, I want to be everything with you. I mean... I just want us to be together. In every way. You know?"

I looked up and tried to reach for him, but he caught my hand. "Will you stop talking?" His blue eyes had softened, and I closed my mouth, waiting. "Now what did you just say?"

My heart beat so fast it hurt. "I said I love you."

He lifted my face to kiss me, and a huge wave of relief rushed through my body. "I heard that part." His lips curved into the smile that melted me every time. "And it's about time you said it."

"I've said it before." I softly touched his lips, remembering the night at the hospital. "You just weren't conscious the first time."

He caught my hand and kissed my finger before lowering both. "But that's not what I meant. Did you say you've never done it before?"

I pushed back and looked down, embarrassed. "If you make fun of me, I'm leaving."

His laugh was as easy as his smile. "But we're at your house."

"Then I'll go to your house." I tried to stand, but he caught my waist.

"I'll just come get you." He pulled me back down against him, and I put my cheek on his bare chest. I couldn't look at him. My heart was still beating too hard.

After a few moments, he spoke. "Is that what you said?"

I nodded, and he leaned back against the wall next to me with an exhale. I slid into his side and under his arm, and we were silent a few moments longer. I chewed my lip, staring at my socks and waiting. Would he leave now? Say it was too much? He couldn't deal with this?

"So all that time, you and Jack never—"

"No." I didn't want to go there. With Jack, it had been over. He'd brought me home.

Julian turned and kissed my head. His arm was across my shoulders. "I don't care. I just always thought he was the problem."

My brow clutched. "In what way?"

"Like he was why you held back. I thought you missed him or something. And really it was—"

"I didn't. I don't miss him." These last few weeks had shown me exactly who I missed and just how much. And he was here beside me.

"C'mon." He stood and pulled me to my feet then led me over to my bed. "Climb in."

I followed him, but my eyes flickered to my door. "Here?"

He shook his head. "I want to think about this one."

My shoulders dropped along with my heart. "You're not into it now."

He shook his head. "It's not that."

"You think I'm weird."

"I think you're great. I just need to think." He studied my frown and laughed, pulling me close. "Would you just trust me here? I have more experience."

I sat on the bed and watched as he picked up the large bear I'd thrown on the floor. "And who's this guy?"

"Mr. Bear?" I took the stuffed toy and put it back in the corner.

"Is he trying to take my place?"

"He might've," I smiled. "But he's not very good at it."

"I'd kick his ass, but I think he outweighs me."

Julian sat on the bed facing me, and I looked at my hands in my lap. Now I felt stupid for even saying anything. He reached forward and pushed a curl back. "I missed you."

I leaned into his arms, and he hugged me, filling my chest with that familiar warmth. "So we're not broken up now?" I asked quietly.

"I'd say no, but you're the hold-out."

"In that case, we're definitely back together."

He kissed my lips, and we slowly lay back on the bed. Then he turned me and pulled me against him, my back to his chest like always. A few minutes went by, and I began to relax as he softly stroked my arm. I felt him chuckle.

"What?" I tilted my head in his direction. He tightened his arms around me and kissed my cheek.

"I was just thinking about you in algebra class last year."

"And you're laughing. Thanks."

"I'm laughing because I couldn't get over you."

I rolled around to face him. "What does that mean?"

"Well, there you were with these cute curls and those green eyes, and I was totally diggin it. But you'd come in with your head down, go to your desk and hide behind your algebra book. Like it was your happy place." He kissed my nose. "I had to ask to borrow your notes every single day to get you to look at me. Then you finally started talking to me."

"And who had to repeat algebra?" I pretended to scold. "You should've been paying more attention to the teacher."

"No way." He smoothed back my hair. "You were far more interesting. What were you so afraid of?"

My brows pulled together. "I wasn't afraid of anything."

"But you never looked around. Our desks were right beside each other then too, remember?" I nodded. "And you would *not* look at me."

Chewing my lip, I debated telling him what a massive crush I had on him. How I couldn't look at him because my face turned beet red whenever I did. How I wanted to die every time he spoke to me, but at the time, my best friend had called dibs. Not that it mattered. Back then, I never believed I had a chance with Julian. It was still a little hard to believe.

"Have you ever considered I was trying to avoid you?" I teased. "You were always talking to me, and you clearly had no grasp of the subject matter."

He rolled me onto my back and kissed me deeply. I felt a familiar flash of desire from my throat down to my toes. As he gently released me, I tried to remember how I'd ever been able to hold back from him. There was nothing like being in his arms, even if it was only until he slipped out again before daylight.

"What was that for?" I asked, slightly breathless.

"I loved you then," he smiled. "And then you got me in the paper and everyone started calling wanting my stuff. I knew we had to be together."

"But I didn't see you that whole summer." I remembered those days leading up to August, and how he'd disappeared.

"I was working." He shrugged. "And I didn't have any money to take you anywhere."

My eyes narrowed. "I know better than that. You were running around."

He breathed a chuckle. "I was only seventeen. I might've found you, but I wasn't going to bank on it."

"Thanks."

"And in August, that first day back, nothing had changed. There you were in the parking lot, clutching your books." His hand went to my waist and he pulled me closer. "You know you were doing it again these last few days."

I couldn't stop my lips pulling down. "I don't want to think about these last few days. They've been awful."

He smiled and kissed my nose. "Yeah, being apart sucked. Bad."

I thought about that first day in the parking lot last fall. He'd suggested we go out then, and I'd been stunned and confused—I was sure I'd misunderstood him. Now I knew we probably would've gotten together if Jack hadn't come along. I put my arms around his neck and hugged him close.

"I was thinking how great it would be if you came to Savannah with me," he said.

My arms loosened and I pulled back so I could see his eyes. "But what about college? Is there even a school in Savannah? I mean, other than the art school?"

"There's Savannah State University."

"Really?" My brow creased.

"Yes. Really." He smiled and moved the side of my hair back.

My eyes blinked around as my mind tripped through the possibilities. "I hadn't even thought about it."

"I know."

I lowered my arms feeling guilty. The end of the year had been depressing because I knew we'd be separated. On top of all that, I'd been distracted by his dad and the secret and our growing relationship...

"I'm sorry," I whispered. "I really am. I honestly hadn't wanted to think about college, and then when this thing came through with Loyola... Rachel's been talking about it so much, I guess it was sort-of decided in my mind."

He nodded. "We never talked about options."

I reached forward and slid my finger down his cheek. "You know, if it hadn't been for all your art school plans, I would've completely spaced and just ended up going somewhere around here."

"All my art school plans?"

I nodded. "When I saw how on top of things you were last year, I felt like a slacker."

"As in, if the bum who fails algebra is planning for college already..."

I giggled. "Something like that."

We were quiet again, and that heaviness pressed on my chest. I wanted to change everything now. "It's just so late," I said, "and I've got to have some kind of financial aid or something..."

"We'll figure it out." He leaned forward and brushed a kiss over my lips. I felt a flush of warmth at the gesture. He pulled back and was serious again, looking right in my eyes. "But you've got to tell me stuff, Anna. It won't work if I feel like you're hiding things from me."

I hesitated, chewing my lip, thinking about the biggest secret of all I was hiding. He interrupted my thoughts with another kiss. "I love you," he whispered.

"I know," I whispered back, still distracted.

He let out a short one-syllable laugh.

"What?" I blinked to him.

"Nothing. Get some rest."

I turned back into our spooning position. "Oh, and they're hazel," I said.

His mouth nuzzled into my shoulder, sparking a little shiver. "What?"

"My eyes. They're hazel."

"They're usually green."

"It's because of the clothes I wear. But if you're my boyfriend, you really should know the color of my eyes."

"Can I call you Hazel?"

"Not if you expect me to answer."

He laughed and pulled me closer. I smiled and snuggled into his arms. It was so wonderful to have him back.

Chapter 18

The next morning, he was gone. I quickly flipped over and grabbed my phone, scrolling to his face.

A groggy voice spoke on the other end. "Hello?"

"I love you!" I said.

"What time is it?" Julian asked, but I could hear him smile.

"I have no idea." I closed my eyes and imagined he was still here. "But I love you."

He laughed then, and I beamed. "What are you doing today?" I asked.

"Mmm... Church?"

My eyes popped open. "Seriously?"

"No." I heard him breathe, and it sounded like he was getting up. "Mom's already left."

"She goes?"

"Every weekend, Saturday or Sunday mass."

My brow furrowed as I thought about that. "I wonder if she sees Lucy and B.J."

"They go?" It sounded like he opened and closed a drawer. "They probably go to St. Thomas. It's way closer to Hammond Island."

"Maybe. But Lucy spends a lot of time with B.J. now." I couldn't tell him his mother wouldn't be disappearing so much if Lucy were staying at home.

"Well, I'm meeting Blake to help him finish up that truck he's working on. Want to come?"

"Nope."

He laughed, and I threw back my covers. Knowing he'd be away from home, I felt like it was my chance. "Is your mom's shop going to be open today?"

"Not til after lunch. You planning to drop by?"

I pulled open a drawer and pulled out my cargo capris. "Maybe. I don't know. Hey, have fun with Blake. And I love you!"

I heard him smiling. "I know, I know."

I grinned and hung up the phone. This was perfect. I could go over, shop, and try to convince his mother that the best graduation gift she could give her son would be the truth.

Ms. LaSalle's store was full of shoppers and crafters when I arrived. Spring break was the start of high season, and all the shops and streets would get busier and more crowded through September.

When I walked in, she smiled cautiously at me, but I gave her a friendly grin in response and she relaxed. I didn't want her to be on guard when we talked, and apart from Julian's art reception, it was the first time we had been alone since our confrontation with Mr. Kyser. That was when she'd offered to do the story with Nancy, and I'd promised never to tell Julian what I knew.

I walked around the shop looking at the beautiful hand-made jewelry hanging on little pegs. Julian had been stringing a turquoise necklace the last time I was here, and he'd made a comment about this place being overwhelming to some people. I was definitely one of those people. I preferred the other side of the store that held the local art and unique souvenirs. I was definitely at a loss when it came to jewelry making. Too many choices and little pieces.

Ms. LaSalle, however, was in her element, leaning over the group of ladies, who were clearly together, and helping them with their final decisions on necklaces and earrings. Her dark hair was swept up in a high ponytail that hung in a single fat braid down her back. Occasionally, it slid around her shoulder, and as usual, she appeared so beautiful and young. I imagined Mr. Kyser must be in heaven now that they were back together.

After a few minutes, the clutch of shoppers had made their decisions and were settling up. They collected their receipts and walked to the door calling back to Ms. LaSalle with delighted exclamations and promises to return again soon. She smiled and waved goodbye. Then she walked over to where I was standing.

"Hey, Anna," she said. "Sorry I couldn't really talk earlier."

"Oh, that's okay," I smiled, putting the necklace I'd been holding back on a peg. "I know how it is."

Her expression was curious, but guarded. "I think Julian's down at Blake's."

I nodded. "I talked to him this morning."

"You two are getting closer it seems. Julian never really talked about anyone before he met you."

My heart filled at her words. "I think... I... well. I love him."

I'd never said it to a person's parent before—I'd never said it to anyone—and I wasn't sure how she was going to respond. She simply blinked a little smile. "So are you looking for something?"

"Not really," I said, not wanting to tell her I was looking for her.

She looked around, and only two people were now in the store. "Well, I'm ready for a break. Want to walk down to the beach with me?"

"Yes!"

"Cheryl?" she called to the girl behind the register. "Will you be okay if I just step out for a few minutes?"

"Oh, sure, Ms. Lex."

We turned and walked toward the door. I followed her down the ramp that led to the parking lot and then across the two-lane beach road. We quickly dashed through the parking lot of an old condominium development and through the posts blocking the pavement from where the sand began. Ms. LaSalle kicked off her sandals and strolled out to the water with me close behind her.

"It's a perfect day," she smiled, crossing her arms over her chest. "If a little chilly."

I fell in beside her walking east at the water's edge.

"So what's up, Anna? I get the feeling something's on your mind."

My hands got clammy, and I wasn't sure how to start with what I wanted to say. "I guess I should forget a career in poker," I said.

"Well, you're not shopping, you're not looking for Julian..."

"Promise you'll hear me out and not get angry?"

"Nope."

I exhaled a nervous laugh. "Will you try?"

She glanced at me and pursed her lips. "What is it?"

"Well, I told you I love Julian," I started carefully.

"So do I." Her voice adopted that sharp tone I knew very well, but I had to push past her walls.

"Right," I said. "But I bet he talks to me more now. I mean, just because we're together a lot and all."

"And?"

"And well, I was just wondering if you've thought anymore about telling him the truth."

"No."

Her tone silenced me for a second. It was her same old response, the same one she'd used with me, the one

I'd heard from her at Mr. Kyser's house. And if she wouldn't give in to him. After that…

"I know you love Julian. I do." I wasn't sure how she would take what I was about to say. "But, Ms. LaSalle, he really needs to know his dad. It's bothering him. It's on his mind a lot, and it's starting to affect his confidence."

Her brow creased, and I could tell she was ready to defend. "Julian is the most confident kid I know."

"He acts that way, but the truth is, he feels…" *What was the right word?* "Insecure about things."

"Like what?" She didn't believe me.

I thought about the day last fall, when he'd said his dad never gave a shit. I remembered that night after his show, how he'd doubted everything. "Like his future… His art."

She stopped walking and crossed her arms. "How would knowing his father matter to his art?"

"I don't know. But he said to me that he was feeling like… like he was a nobody."

She smiled and dropped her arms, walking again but at a slower pace. "All artists go through that when they're starting out. He'll get through it, and once he's in Savannah, everything'll change for him."

"I'm sure you're right for the most part, but there's his classmates, too."

She stopped walking again. "Do kids make fun of him?"

"No! Not at all, but some of the guys make comments about you, and —"

"About me?"

"Not anything rude," I stammered. "Actually, they're very complimentary. Saying they want to ask you out and stuff."

She seemed to relax. "Boys like to talk big. Your mother's very pretty. They probably say things like that about her, and your father is clearly identified."

I raised my eyebrows remembering Julian used to be Mom's most vocal fan. This conversation was not going how I'd wanted. "But Ms. LaSalle—"

"Now listen to me." Her voice was firm, but her face was gentle. "I really like you Anna, and I really like that Julian likes you. I think he genuinely cares about you, and you seem to feel the same way."

"I do—"

"But I don't want my son to be a Kyser."

My mouth dropped open. *That* was not what I expected. "But he is a Kyser."

"Only by blood," she said. "And even then only half. The other half's mine, and I hope it's stronger."

Never in a million years would I have expected that response, and while I sort of understood where she was coming from, it was completely unfair and not a good enough excuse. *She* was obviously in love with a Kyser, and maybe their family had issues, but all of the issues could be traced back to one big thing—The Secret. And lying and sneaking around wasn't helping anyone heal.

"I don't know which half is stronger," I said, "but I do know neither would want to be lied to."

She stopped walking and stared out at the ocean. Then she took a deep breath and sat on the sand wrapping her arms around her knees. I sat down facing her.

"Julian is confident and happy," she said. "He has no idea Bill's his father, and I want it to stay that way."

"But you love Mr. Kyser!" I bit my lip hoping I hadn't gone too far.

Her eyes dropped, and for a moment she didn't speak. Then with a little nod from her, I started to breathe again.

"I do love him," she said quietly. "I love him very much. But Bill's... he's not the type of influence I want in my son's life."

I was amazed. Somehow we'd made it to a place we'd never been—a place more open. It gave me hope. I started to say more, but she cut me off.

"You know his children. You've seen how they are. I don't want Julian becoming like that. I don't want him growing ruthless. Or angry. Or depressed."

"Have you ever considered that could change?" I said quietly, carefully. "The problems with Will and Jack and Lucy... well, it's because of what happened to their mom."

Ms. LaSalle shook her head. "It's more than that."

"Yes, it's because their dad completely shut down. He blocked them all out and did nothing but blame himself and long for you."

Ms. LaSalle looked at me strangely. "What do you know about it?"

"I... well, I..." *Heck!* She didn't know I'd read the journals. "I just guessed that's how it went. I mean, it seems that way—"

"Anna, you don't know Bill like I do. Even when he was your age, he was so focused and determined. His personality is so strong." She looked in the distance. "Meg was no match for him."

"But he's different when he's with you. I've seen him. And it would be different if you were together."

She didn't reply, and we were quiet for several seconds just listening to the waves break on the shore. It really was a beautiful, chilly day.

183

"I'm sure losing their mom hurt Bill's children," she finally said. "But the money, the power, all of that plays a part in who they are. And a big part of who Julian is comes from his independence. He doesn't have to live up to anyone's expectations."

"But that's what's bothering him," I said. "Not knowing who he is causes him to doubt what he can be."

She shook her head. "I've already told you what I think about that. Right now he's going through a huge transition. It's scary, and he's nervous. But Julian will be fine."

I couldn't argue with her anymore. Clearly, I wasn't going to change her mind today.

"We've got to get back!" She jumped up and dusted off her skirt. Then she turned, and I followed her back in the direction we'd come.

"Yeah, I've got to get home anyway," I said.

She paused a moment, and I could tell she was choosing her words. "Please trust me, Anna. I love Julian, and I only want what's best for him."

"But you're wrong." I said softly. "And I love him, too. And you're asking me to lie to him. You of all people should know how that makes me feel. The position it puts me in."

"I'm sorry you found out." She shook her head. "But the truth would hurt him so much worse. You have to trust me."

I frowned, and she gave me a brief hug. Then she turned and quickly went into the shop. I stood beside my car in the parking lot thinking about her son and wishing I could see him. Ms. LaSalle was the most frustrating person. Mr. Kyser had a strong personality? That was a joke coming from her. I'd never met anyone so stubborn. Finally, I gave up and drove home.

Chapter 19

Mom was balancing a large coffee cake and running out the door as I was running in. "Dinner's in the microwave," she called breathlessly and kissed my cheek.

"Where are you going?"

"Miranda called in sick, and I've got to run over to work the register at the association office."

The art association was also a working gallery, and with the start of high season, they were as busy as everyone.

"Will you be late?" I asked.

"Shopping ends at seven, and then I'll just have to close up the register and shut everything down."

"Where's dad?"

"He had to check on some problem at a job site." She stood in the door looking frustrated by all my questions.

"I'm sorry. I'll be fine." I said, waving my hands. "Take off."

"You sure?" She paused, the cake still balanced. "You could come and help. I know it's tough being alone with the breakup and all."

"Oh! I didn't tell you! We got back together!"

Now she was coming back inside. "Did you do what I said? Tell him how you felt?"

"Yes! And it worked. He..." I couldn't tell her he'd spent the night. "We decided we really wanted to be together."

"That's great, hon. I really like Julian. Now, I've got to run!" She turned and opened the door again, dashing out. "I'll talk to you tonight!"

The house was silent, so I walked over to the couch, picking up my phone. I touched his profile, expecting voicemail. My heart jumped when he answered. I could hear his smile, which made me smile, too.

"Are you calling to say you love me again?" he asked.

"Yes," I said. "And I'm home alone. And I miss you."

"Where's your hot mom?" His voice strained in a way that sounded like he was lifting something.

"She has to work til seven and then shut down."

"And Dad?"

"Some problem on a job site."

"I'm still at Blake's, but I could be over in a half hour."

"Sounds great." I hung up the phone and ran upstairs to shower. I had just enough time to pick out a cute dress and freshen my makeup when I heard his car outside. I ran downstairs as he tapped on the door.

"Different perspective coming through the door," he smiled pulling me into his arms. I slid my hands up his shoulders and he leaned down to kiss me. His soft lips touching mine made every part of me feel electric.

"Julian?" I whispered.

"Hm?" he kissed my cheek, my forehead.

"Mom's idea of dinner was a hot pocket."

He chuckled and raised his head to look at me. "I love those!"

I shook my head. "We are not splitting a hot pocket."

"C'mon. I'll buy you dinner."

"You don't have to—"

"I want to." He smiled, pulling me out the door to his car, and we jumped in and drove to ZaZa's at the

Intercoastal marina. It wasn't as packed as it was going to be when tourist season got going, and we were able to find a table quickly. I ordered a jerk chicken sandwich while Julian just had a Coke.

My brows pulled together. "You're not hungry?"

"I'll eat your fries."

That made me smile. "Deal. You can have them all."

"So did you drive over to Mom's?" He sipped his drink and grabbed a handful off my plate.

"Yep." I nodded, finishing my bite.

"See anything you liked?"

Shaking my head as I swallowed, I managed to speak. "She didn't have anything of yours on sale."

He smiled. "You know, Mom's pretty good at making jewelry, too."

A few families shared the restaurant with us, and I noticed a dad walking two little boys down to the sandy playground just off the dining area. A live band was playing acoustic classics at the other end of the room, and the lapping of the water against the wall formed a constant backdrop. I watched Julian's eyes follow the man with his sons.

"How'd it go with Blake?" I interrupted his thoughts.

"I'm thinking about buying that truck from him."

"What?" I frowned.

"It makes more sense for moving stuff and taking pieces to galleries, and my car's about had it." He tossed a fry at me. "You don't want to date me without the convertible?"

"Please. I don't care what you drive." But I was thinking about my BMW ruse. "Have you made a deal with him?"

"Nah, it's just something I'm thinking about. He wants to fix it up to sell. Get some extra cash. I might not be able to give him what he wants for it."

Julian was still watching the father with his sons. I looked over at them. They were a cute family, and it was obvious the little boys adored their dad. I was worried about what he might be thinking.

"You ready?" I said.

"You done?" He inspected my half-eaten sandwich.

I laughed. "I don't want to eat up all our time together."

"Good one." He grabbed a big bite of my dinner.

"I thought you weren't hungry!"

He shrugged. "ZaZa's is expensive."

My heart sank. "We didn't have to come here."

"I figured you're used to going out to nice places."

"Julian…" I reached across the table for his hand.

"What?"

"Jack and I only went out to dinner once."

He didn't meet my eyes. "I wasn't thinking about him."

"No? Who else have I dated?"

He shrugged, standing and holding the back of my chair. "You did other stuff."

I stood and kissed his cheek. "I love you."

"Let's get out of here." He put cash on the table, and we left the restaurant.

Driving home, I slid across the seat and put my head on his shoulder.

"You really should be safer," he said.

"I know. I was just thinking about how restrictive seatbelts are." I kissed the side of his neck, and he wrapped an arm around my shoulders. It was the

---

188

greatest ride home ever, but sadly, when we pulled into my driveway, my dad's truck was there.

"Great," I exhaled.

Julian laughed. "Poor dad. Want me to come in or just come back later?"

I shrugged. "It's up to you."

"Let me head on home. I need to check in with Mom."

I slipped my hand up to his cheek and kissed him softly. Our lips parted, and when his tongue touched mine, every part of me heated up. He gently pulled back, and our eyes met, his that cool Kyser blue. I'd thought I loved Jack, but I had never felt this way about anyone before. Julian knew me so well, and even though he made my stomach tighten into knots every time he smiled at me, they were thrilling knots. Yet somehow, at the same time, I was completely at ease with him.

"Back soon," he whispered.

I walked into the house and Dad was at the bar eating the hot pocket Mom had left in the microwave. "Where have you been?" he asked.

"Julian took me to ZaZa's."

Dad frowned. "I thought Mom said you two broke up."

"We did, but we got back together."

He nodded. "He's a good kid."

"I think so." I watched him take another big bite of the sandwich. "Hey, Dad? What would you do if..." I wasn't sure how to phrase it without giving away too much information.

His brow creased. He put down the hot pocket and faced me. "If what?"

"Well," I hesitated, "say you knew somebody who was keeping a secret from somebody else. And you really wanted them to tell the other person, but they wouldn't."

"Not much you can do about that. Who's keeping a secret?"

I shrugged. "Just one of my girlfriends. And I think the person needs to know the truth, but I can't convince her to tell him."

He pressed his lips together briefly. "Is it something dangerous?"

I shook my head. "No."

"Is someone going to get hurt?"

"Not physically."

"Then you're just going to have to let it play out."

I frowned. "But it's the wrong decision."

"Then she'll have to deal with the consequences."

I didn't like the sound of that. I hugged Dad and made an excuse to go upstairs. After a while, Mom stuck her head in my room to say goodnight, and a little while later the entire house was quiet. I glanced at the clock and realized Julian would be here before long.

Running over to my dresser, I dug out the cutest sleep set I owned then I smoothed my hair and touched a little perfume on my neck. I smiled, feeling self-conscious. I'd never done any of these things for him before.

Still, I turned on my music player and adjusted the volume to low then I slid into bed and picked up a book. I had fallen asleep when I felt him slide in behind me, but my heart jumped. I quickly moved into his arms.

"Hey," he whispered. I didn't speak, but rather scooted up to kiss him. He rolled me onto my back and kissed me slowly. Our lips moved against each others', and my whole body felt tingly and warm. A small noise came from my throat as his hands slid under my shirt.

Chills followed his fingers across my stomach, traveling higher, until he discovered I wasn't wearing a bra. He made a pleased sound, and my arms tightened around his neck.

Pressure was building inside me with every touch, and I pulled desperately at the thin sweater he wore. He quickly took it off and returned to me, but my hands weren't satisfied. They went under the tee he was wearing, I wanted his skin. But as soon as I touched him, he let out a frustrated groan. He kissed my mouth one more time before sitting up and shoving his fingers into the sides of his hair, propping his elbows on his bent knees. I frowned and pulled up beside him, straightening my top.

"What's wrong?" I whispered.

He shook his head but didn't speak.

"What is it?" My whisper grew more urgent. I wanted him back. I wanted to keep doing what we were doing.

"I can't do this," he said, jaw clenched. I watched as he slid to the floor and leaned back against my bed.

I dropped down beside him, my body still throbbing. "I don't understand. We've been doing this for months."

"Yeah, but it's different now."

My lips tightened, and I reached for his shoulder. I wouldn't let him pull away like this. I wanted him to kiss me again.

He looked at me. "I want it be special for you. Not like this, here, with your parents right across the hall."

"Julian..." I moved to my knees and put my hands on his cheeks to kiss him. He lowered his knees and pulled me into his chest, but after a few more kisses, he moved me beside him and stood.

"I'd better go," he said.

"Why?" I jumped up to follow him, grabbing a fistful of his shirt.

"Listen," he said, stopping at the window. "The first time's different. You're going to remember it. I *want* you to remember it. You're my angel, and I want it to be the best thing we share."

My hand dropped. "I do, too, but... well, it'll be memorable no matter what."

"Nope." He smoothed a curl behind my ear. "I want it to be better than that."

"Julian. Stay with me." I pleaded. "I don't want you to go."

He pulled me into a hug and kissed my head. "I know. I'll figure something out soon."

He let me go and was out the window before I could stop him. I watched him descend, and at the bottom he looked up and smiled. For some reason, the balcony scene from *Romeo and Juliet* was in my head. What had they said about parting being sweet sorrow? I always thought that was a dumb line. Not anymore. I knew exactly what they meant. Except I'd ditch the sweet part altogether. It was only sorrow.

I gazed after him jogging down the road as long as I could until he disappeared from sight. Then I walked back to my bed, kicking a shoe across the room on my way. His sweater was on my floor, so I picked it up and pulled it over my head. It smelled like him. I carried Mr. Bear to the bed to lay behind me, and this time his huge paw around my waist combined with the warm scent of Julian's sweater almost made me feel better. After about ten minutes, I grabbed my phone and punched up his number.

"Hey," Julian said. "It's really cold tonight."

"You left your sweater." I closed my eyes, imagining my cheek pressed against his chest.

"I realized it when I hit the ground."

"You could've come back for it."

"I might not've left."

"That would've been okay."

"Anna…" He exhaled a sigh, and for a moment we didn't speak.

I broke the silence with a sad little whisper. "I miss you. We've been apart two weeks. We got one night, and now this."

"I know," he chuckled. "I'm pretty sure I've lost it. I'm about to turn the car around and come back."

I sat up quick, my voice excited. "Do it!"

He laughed again. "Next night Mom's away, can you make up an excuse and come to my house?"

"Like what?" I asked, thinking.

"I don't know. Spend the night with Rachel or something?"

My mind raced through all our options. "We're out of school all week. Maybe I could come over one afternoon?"

"I told Mom I'd help her at the store every day til school starts back."

"Why'd you do that?"

"We were broke up."

I sighed. "Well, I guess this is it, then. It was nice while it lasted."

Julian laughed. "Okay, hot pants. I would think after eighteen years you'd be more patient. I'm the one who knows what I'm missing."

I lay back down, pulling Mr. Bear's arm back over me. "I bet you didn't make such a production out of your first time." Then my mind wandered. "Who was it?"

"You know, it's not cool to talk about exes." I heard the door slam, and I realized he was back at his house.

"Do you have any exes?"

"Not really."

"Oh my god." The sudden realization put a lump in my throat.

"What?"

My eyes pressed closed. "It was Renee, wasn't it? Were you hers?"

"This is why talking about exes isn't such a great idea."

"Do you consider Renee one of your exes?"

"No."

"Why not?" I felt a flash of jealousy again. "Is she still a possibility?"

His voice was a whisper, and I figured he was inside his house. "Are you trying to trick me?"

"You were just with her at the bonfire."

"And I left her there to be with you."

I thought about what happened that night. They were on a date, and yes, he'd left her to come to my house. But *how* had he left her? "Did she think you two were together as a couple?"

"I don't think Renee thinks of me that way."

"I think you're wrong."

"Well, even if I am, I don't think of her that way."

I remembered her sitting on his work table, neckline plunging. "She is just so... so..."

Julian laughed. "You don't have to be jealous of Renee."

"She is *always* waiting for you."

"She's really not."

"Oh, please." I rolled my eyes. "I saw her clutching your arm. She's like a vulture. Or a —"

194

"Hey, know what?"

"What?"

"I love you."

I bit my lip. "I love you, too."

"And I'm home now. So you give that imagination a rest, okay?"

"You're working tomorrow?"

"Yep. But I'll call you when I get off."

"OK. 'Night."

"Night."

We hung up the phone, and I rolled onto my back and stared at the ceiling. I really hated Renee Barron. I thought about her black hair and green eyes a few seconds longer. Then I pulled the neck of Julian's sweater over my nose to breathe in his scent. Mr. Bear's arm was around me, and I closed my eyes to sleep.

Chapter 20

Spring break turned unexpectedly long and boring and difficult. Nancy was out of town, so the paper office was dead. The first day, I went in, but after sitting around doing nothing until lunch, I drove to Ms. LaSalle's shop. Julian was working, and the customer flow was pretty much nonstop.

He was very patient helping tourists make their own jewelry, and I wandered around watching him sprint between answering questions and handling the register. I'd have been happy watching him all day, but I felt in the way. So I made an excuse and left. That evening I was ready to see him when he texted asking if I'd meet him at our regular stretch of beach.

We walked out to the water holding hands as the sun faded into the ocean. It was so wonderful being with him, feeling his warm fingers laced with mine. At the shoreline, he sat on the sand. I sat behind him, straddling my legs down his sides and resting my cheek on his back. I wrapped my arms around his waist and felt his palms slide down the back of my calves to my ankles, stopping at my bare feet.

"I really love you," I said, listening to his heartbeat through his back. I heard him chuckle. "It's amazing."

"Yeah," he said.

I had closed my eyes in the dim orange light, but I could still see the flash of the camera as it went off.

"Got it!" Summer called out. "Good one."

I lifted my head. "What are you doing here?"

"Practicing my photography. Check it out," she said turning her large camera around to show me the snapshot of Julian and me. "That's the yearbook shot. Cutest couple. No?"

"Over Rachel and Brad?" I argued. "You're joking, right?"

"No way! You guys are totally it. Besides, you've been the soap opera of senior year. Especially after Renee's meltdown when Julian ditched her at the bonfire Saturday to find you."

I felt a little warmth around my middle. Julian didn't say anything, but he stood and walked down to the water.

"What was that all about?" Summer asked.

I watched him, feeling irresistibly smug. I would've loved to witness that scene.

"Nothing," I said. "Just you again."

"Sorry." Summer looked down, but then she glanced up at me. We both grinned.

"I'm sorry I left you there," I said. "I was majorly depressed. But you got home all right?"

"Oh, yeah," she said. "And I didn't care. I wouldn't have missed that drama for the world. Looks like it turned out all right for you, too."

"Yeah," I said. Julian was walking slowly, but I knew he'd wanted us to have some alone time. "I'd better catch up with him, but send me a copy of that picture."

"You got it," she called after me.

There was a time when Julian and I were easy together. We would joke and laugh all the way to the car, all the way through the drive to wherever we were going, then all the way through whatever event we were attending. We would spend the whole night in my bed with his arm around my waist, his soft breath on my neck. And we would sleep…

Now all that was over. Now there was this force between us. A longing that kept us in a constant state of distraction. I couldn't put my finger on when the switch had flipped, but the tension every time we were together now was almost overwhelming.

Julian planned all our dates with plenty of activity, but we were both silently watching for any chance we'd get to be alone. It was starting to wear me out, and I imagined how this week might've gone had he not been working at his mom's store. Then I thought of rabbits.

Friday we'd planned to see a movie. Our date started with our new routine—I got in the car, and he glanced at me and smiled. It was like lightening shooting through me, all the way to my toes. I smiled back before quickly looking down again. I couldn't think of a thing to say. I only wanted to grab him and jump him right there on the spot.

We drove in silence, but instead of heading to the theater, he took me to the Romar Beach pavilion. The public lot was empty after dark, and by the time he'd killed the engine, I was out of my seatbelt and in his arms.

Our kisses were even different now. I couldn't catch my breath, and my heart was pounding in my ears. My eyes were closed, and I was reaching, kissing any part of him I could find. His lips traveled from my jaw to my neck, and I heard myself make a little sound like a yelp. It was all heat and pounding and trying to pull him closer to me than was humanly possible. Until he leaned back, holding me away from him by my shoulders, eyes closed. We were both breathing heavily.

"We've got to do something," he said in a hoarse whisper.

"I agree," I leaned toward him, but he stopped me.

"Not that."

"Julian…" I pleaded.

"I shouldn't have brought us here." He wouldn't look at me. "We should go to the movie. Or some place with lots of lights. And people."

I slid my hand down to his stomach, but he caught my wrist. "Seriously, Anna. Your first time's not going to be in a damn car."

My eyes closed, and I lightly placed my forehead on his cheek. "How can you be this way all of a sudden?"

"I don't like it either." He calmed his breathing. "But what you've done is special."

"I'm tired of being special." I kissed his cheek, lightly moving my lips over his skin, back toward his mouth. "I want to be with you."

"Dammit." He slid me off his lap with a groan, turning back to face the steering wheel. For a minute he didn't say anything then he let out a deep exhale. "That's kind of been on my mind, too."

I reached over and ran my finger down his lined upper arm, imagining it wrapped around my bare body. I shivered. "What's on your mind?"

His eyes met mine. "You're special. And you want to be with me."

My brow lined, and I moved my hand from his arm toward his stomach. "So? I love you."

He guided my wrist around his waist and pulled me into a hug. With my head on his chest, I could hear his heart pounding as fast as mine.

"I love you, too," he said. "But well, I've got nothing over here. I'm gambling on everything, and I can't make any promises to you. I don't even know who I am—"

I sat up fast, glaring. "Oh my god."

"What?"

"Is this about not knowing who your dad is?"

"I know that's getting old…"

I slid across the seat, threw open my door, and stomped out of the car, headed to the water.

"OH MY GOD!" I yelled into the black night. Then I ran hard, all the way to the shore, and spun around. "Are you KIDDING ME?!" I yelled up at Phoenician V or VI or whichever the hell one was towering over us.

"Anna, shhh!" Julian ran up and grabbed my arm.

"I QUIT!" I yelled at the giant tower of concrete. "Do you hear me? This is IT!"

"Seriously. Anna." Julian forced me to look at him. "You're scaring the tourists."

I jerked out of his hands and stomped away, down the water's edge. Julian trotted up behind me laughing. "So why are you yelling at the high rises again?"

"Wouldn't you like to know," I grumbled.

"Yes. That's why I asked."

"Julian." I stopped walking and looked at him. His blue eyes shone, and I shook my head. I couldn't do it. I'd promised. And I hated that promise right now with every fiber of my being. "I don't care about your family or who your dad is." That was true at least. "I love you. You're special to me, and I want to be with you."

He took both my hands in his. "I care."

"I know."

Lowering himself to the dry sand facing the black Gulf, he pulled me next to him, stroking the inside of my arm.

201

No one was around, and I lay my head on his shoulder.

"I was just thinking if I had a little more time," he said. "Maybe, I don't know. Maybe I could get you a ring or something."

"A ring?" Pressure was building behind my eyes.

"I know. It sounds nuts, but it feels different with us now. More serious, more like something important."

"We're not old enough to be making those kinds of decisions," I sighed, thinking of his dad's advice.

"Are you even on the pill?" he looked down at me.

Speaking of his dad! "No." I was suddenly embarrassed. "I guess haven't done my homework."

"That wasn't really my point, but I'm glad I asked." He sighed and looked out at the water. "I just... I really love you, and I want everything to be good for you."

"It's great," I said, squeezing his hand. "We've been building to this for years. And you did give me a ring."

He looked at me, and I couldn't stop. I pulled his face to mine and pressed our lips together. It was an insistent kiss. I wasn't letting him go, but I didn't have to. He pulled me toward him and we were back in the place we'd been in the car, hands searching, bodies drawn together like magnets, wanting everything all at once. But again he pulled up for air.

"I'm not marrying you, Julian." I wailed, dropping my head to his chest.

"Never?" he laughed, lifting my chin.

"Not in the next five years. So if you're planning to make me wait that long, you can just forget it."

"You're breaking up with me over sex? Isn't that supposed to be my deal?"

"Stop it." I pulled my face away.

I wanted to cry. I'd never felt so desperate in my life. My whole body was on fire, and it hurt. "I just want you to touch me."

I took his hands and slid them to my waist under my shirt. I pressed my mouth to his and for a moment, his fingers traveled lightly up my back to my bra. Hesitating, they continued around, cupping the front under my shirt.

I was drowning again as I slid my hand to his waist, finding his skin at the edge of his jeans. I pulled up the soft fabric of his tee and lightly touched his stomach.

Suddenly he was gone. My lips were still in a pucker, and he was down at the water away from me. I watched as he stripped off his shirt and slipped out of his jeans before diving into the dark Gulf waters.

I fell forward, laying my head on my forearm in the sand. "I'm going to kill your parents," I sighed, watching him come out of the surf again in his boxers and rub his hands quickly through is hair, throwing water everywhere.

He pulled his shirt back on and jerked his jeans up over his wet body. "That actually works," he said, walking up to me and helping me stand. The drops of water that hit me were like ice.

"What?" I asked.

"The whole cold shower trick. Come on."

"Where are we going?"

"Somewhere... not here."

As we drove back toward Fairview, I watched him under the passing streetlights. I turned sideways in the seat to face him, my knees pulled to my chest. My head was leaning back against the seat, and I remembered that first night in my bedroom when he had pulled my shirt up so fast and covered my breasts with burning kisses. I closed my eyes and shivered. To have a do-over of *that* night...

I remembered the sensation of his skin against mine and how he'd held me. How could he be so restrained now? I couldn't figure it out. I kept remembering his body curled up behind me in my small bed. It had been so wonderful when I could drift to sleep knowing he'd be there until the early hours. I could feel his breathing, his warm arm around my waist...

I lifted my head, and we were sitting in my driveway in the car. Julian had slid over next to me, and he was sitting with his feet on the dash and his arm around behind my head. I'd fallen asleep for who knows how long.

"I'm sorry," I said, sitting up groggy.

He slid a curl off my cheek. "I miss watching you sleep."

"Come inside," I pleaded. "Spend the night."

"Nope," he grinned.

I exhaled and sat all the way up grabbing the door handle and pushing the heavy door open. I stomped all the way to my front door, Julian right behind me.

"Don't be a baby," he said.

"I just don't get it, Julian. I don't get you."

"That's really hard for me to accept," he said.

"What?"

"That you suddenly don't get me."

I stood on the step in front of my door, and from that height, I could rest my elbows on his shoulders. He slipped his hands in my back pockets and pulled our bodies together.

"So that's the deal," I said.

"What?"

"I have the ring, you find out who your dad is, and things can go back to the way they were with us?" I leaned forward and kissed him, long and slow. "Plus some extra stuff?"

His hands slid out of my pockets and held my waist for a long pause before he straightened me up on the step. "Sure," he shrugged. "That can be the deal. What did you have in mind?"

"Leave it to me."

His forehead creased. "What are you going to do?"

"Nothing. Get some rest, and I'll talk to you tomorrow." I kissed him lightly and then opened the door.

Looking back, I watched him walk slowly to the T-bird. I had no idea what I planned to do, but at least I had an idea of where to start. I ran to my room and grabbed my ring off the holder on my dresser. This little memento wasn't leaving my finger ever again.

Chapter 21

Somehow being back in school made it easier to keep our hands to ourselves. Teachers like Ms. Harris were probably the reason. We always had to drop the hugs and distance ourselves before resuming our pre-breakup seating arrangement. I couldn't tell if the poor student we kept displacing was simply irritated or really mad. I decided to bake him some cookies or something as an apology token.

"You paid attention those last few weeks in class," Julian whispered as I pulled out my notebook. "You might pass after all."

"Maybe we should break up more often," I teased, looking up at the board.

"No way. I'll be *your* tutor for a change," he winked.

"I know one thing you can teach me."

His eyes gleamed, and he leaned back in his seat that sly grin on his lips. It had been a while since I'd seen it. "Keep that up, and I might forget about our deal."

A little charge raced from my stomach to my toes. "Is that all it takes?"

Sensing a presence, I glanced up to see our teacher standing over me, a stern look on her face. I jumped and returned to solving the word problem from the board. From the corner of my eye, I saw Julian sit forward and do the same.

Lunchtime found us all at our regular spot in the quad with Rachel, Brad, and his entire entourage hanging around. Now Rachel's party-planning had shifted to prom-mode, and it was more intense than ever. My mind traveled to dresses and skirt lengths and possible after-prom activities when Wade walked up with Montage.

"They arrested those guys who jumped you in the parking lot," Wade said, stopping at Brad.

"When?" Brad stood. "Who were they?"

Montage shrugged. "Claim to be random jackasses collecting video for some high school fight club. Said they didn't know who you were."

"What?" Rachel cried. Brad sat down, exhaling in disbelief.

Wade continued. "I don't believe it either, but there's an upside."

"Increased interest in the basketball team?" Julian teased from where he sat with me leaning against his chest.

"Make that two," Wade returned. "Now they know about the guys after Mo."

Montage sat down heavily. "I'm sorry, bro," he said under his breath.

Brad clapped him on the shoulder. "It's all good. They'll find those guys, and then you can rest easy."

"I guess I did take one for the team," Julian joked after lunch as he walked me to class. My phone buzzed, and I pulled it out to see a text from Lucy.

Coffee after school? it said.

"Oh, wow. I haven't talked to Lucy in ages," I said under my breath. "I need to meet up with her."

"I'm still helping Blake with that truck," Julian said. "Take off."

I texted her back that I'd be there. "He should give you a discount on it," I said.

I thought about Mr. Kyser and wondered what the hold up might be. Maybe he was figuring out a way to surprise Julian? Maybe a graduation present? He needed to hurry up.

"I'll tell him you said that." Julian kissed my head and took off.

The Fairview coffee house also specialized in homemade desserts, and Lucy was waiting with a small chocolate cake when I arrived. She was dressed in her field clothes, and I'd never seen her so casual. She wore old jeans and a dirty khaki shirt, but her hair was smoothed up in a pony tail. Her face was made, and she was as beautiful as ever. When I walked in, she hugged me, but something was wrong. Her expression was serious. My mind immediately went to Jack.

"Did something happen?" I asked, fearing what she might say.

"Can you keep a secret?" Her voice dropped low.

You have no idea, I thought. "What kind of secret?"

She took a deep breath and glanced around, then she leaned forward, speaking so softly, I could barely hear her. "Dad's having an affair."

My eyes flew wide and my jaw dropped. I closed it, but I couldn't decide if I should act surprised or what. Then I realized — this could be a way out of my problem!

"What?" I pretended to be shocked.

Her brow lined. "Is *affair* the right word? Or should I just say he's sleeping with someone. I mean, technically he hasn't been married since…"

"What happened?" I urged. I had to know if she'd seen Julian's mom at her house, and if she had, what then?

"I've been spending more time with B.J. since Christmas, and well," she glanced down, "I confess, I haven't been going home as much."

I nodded, trying not to scream *Go on!*

"This morning, I'd run out of jeans, and normally, I'd just skip it and wear a skirt." She picked up her coffee cup and took a sip. "This one time I wore shorts, but that was a disaster. My legs got all scratched up—"

"Lucy!" I cried, unable to help myself.

Her eyebrows went up. "Was I rambling?"

"A little," I tried to laugh and play it off like I wasn't bursting for her to get to the point.

She did a little laugh back. "Well, anyway, I got home, and Dad's room is down from mine, pretty far actually..."

I know, I know! I thought, remembering the morning I'd been there.

"I wasn't meaning to snoop, but the house was so quiet." She sipped her coffee again, and I was sure this was yet another torture test. "I heard laughter, so I walked down the hall, and what do you think I saw?"

I'd just picked up my cup and dared to take a sip of the hot liquid when she stopped speaking and waited, staring at me. I almost spit it back in the cup. "A woman?"

"And not just any woman. She was gorgeous!" She shook her head and looked down. "I suppose I should've expected that."

"Did you recognize her?" I almost couldn't stand it. If Lucy knew they were together, how could they keep it a secret anymore? And then if Julian started coming around, I knew Lucy would figure it out. She had to see it...

The side of her nose curled with a frown. "No," she said. "I don't know who she is. I didn't get a very good look. Her back was to the door, so all I saw was long, dark hair."

I exhaled loudly, my brows pulling together. "But you said she was gorgeous. How could you know if you didn't see her face?"

She sat back, picking up the fork and poking the dark cake. "I could just tell. I've never seen Dad that way in my life."

I snorted a laugh then. "Naked?"

She burst out laughing, too. "Holy shit, no! I would've screamed if I'd seen *that*. They were just talking." She smiled, but her expression changed to thoughtful. "He was just so... happy. And, well..." she paused, a sudden sadness passing over her. "I realized I've never seen my own father happy."

My throat tightened as I watched her eyes grow damp. My own eyes misted, and I leaned forward to catch her hand. "But that's good, yes?"

She pressed her lips into a smile and nodded.

I tried to think of anything. "You said they were talking. Did you hear what they said?"

"Yes," she said, shaking out of it. "It was weird. Dad said she could have Will's old car."

Again, she caught me mid-sip, but this time I inhaled hot liquid into my lungs. I coughed so hard, I had to stand.

"Oh my god, Anna!" Lucy was right at my side beating on my back. I grabbed her arm, struggling to get control.

"What did she say?" I managed to ask, my eyes flooded.

Lucy shrugged. "I didn't stick around to hear. I'm sure she said yes, why wouldn't she? It's practically a brand-new Beemer!"

I swallowed the lump in my throat. Everything was coming to a head now, and the secret was right on the verge of exposure. If Julian showed up in Will's old car and Lucy saw it, would she see what that meant? I was practically shaking when I said my next words.

"When you and Julian were dating—"

"I wouldn't say we dated," she interrupted. "We only talked on the phone a few times, and then I was at his house that night I had the accident…"

"Yes," I jumped in. "That night. Was it just the two of you? I mean, was anybody else at his house?"

"I don't know if anybody was there," she leaned back and sipped her drink. "I didn't see anybody."

For a moment I sat in silence, thinking. Lucy had never met Julian's mom—at least not that she could remember. Clearly, there were no pictures of Ms. LaSalle around the Kyser house, and as I thought back to the reception, they didn't speak. Lucy didn't seem to know her. I wondered if she would even remember Julian's mom from that night in January.

"Why?" she asked. "You're not worried that he and I—"

"Oh, no," I said quickly. "I didn't mean that."

Her brow lined, and she studied her cup. I'd forgotten how smart Lucy was, how much people underestimated her. "Julian has dark hair…" her voice trailed off as she thought, and I felt like I couldn't breathe. "What do you know, Anna?"

My mouth dropped open, but I couldn't say a word. All of the knowledge that was hanging over us felt like a knife that could cut this situation either way. "Nothing," I said quickly, looking down.

Her eyes narrowed. "Julian said his mom owned a little shop in Dolphin Island. Would you take me to it?"

"I don't know." My whole body was tight as a drum with anticipation and fear of the unknown.

"Please?" She looked directly at me with those blue eyes just like her father's, just like all of them. It was the second time I'd seen such determination in her. "I need to know what's going on."

My lips pressed together, and I stood, collecting my bag and keys. She followed me, and we went out to Mom's Civic. I'd bring her back for her car later.

Ms. LaSalle's shop was closed when we arrived, and for a moment, I breathed a sigh of relief. I hadn't had a chance to process what might happen—how much Lucy might already know and how much Julian's mom might think I'd told her.

"I guess we missed her," I started to say, but the words died on my lips. In a swirl of colorful fabric and long, dark hair, Alexandra LaSalle stepped out of her shop into the breezy afternoon and then turned to lock the door.

Lucy made an audible gasp. "It's her." And she was out of the car before I could stop her.

I sat in the car as she first ran to the steps leading up to the shop's porch and then stopped when Julian's mom turned around. Ms. LaSalle froze, her expression stunned as she faced the girl. Lucy's blonde hair blew across her shoulder, and for a moment, they didn't move. My eyes filled with tears at the memory of what I'd read. Lucy had been named for her mother's best friend, and I couldn't help but wonder if this was how Meg might have looked facing her today.

Julian's mom took a cautious step forward, and Lucy didn't budge. She didn't speak or run, and from where I sat, I couldn't tell if any recognition passed over her face. It was only those few moments, however, that space of confrontation suspended in time. I didn't see who spoke first, but words were exchanged, and in two steps, they were in each others arms, hugging. Tears filled my eyes. All those years ago, the last time Ms. LaSalle had seen her best friend was almost at this very spot. Was it possible the love of friendship couldn't be stopped by the barriers of time or injury? Was there a chance those old wounds might still be healed?

They released each other and then laughed, seeming embarrassed by their display of affection. I stepped out of the car and carefully closed my door, not sure if I'd be welcome or not. Lucy glanced back at me and held out her hand.

"This is my friend Anna," she said. "I guess you know her from Julian. I asked her to bring me here."

My eyes were big as I walked toward the two. Ms. LaSalle didn't speak, and I was sure she wondered the extent of Lucy's knowledge and how much I'd said.

"She saw you at the house this morning," I said quickly.

Her face flushed pink, and she turned to Lucy. "I'm sorry," she stammered.

"Please don't!" Lucy cried. "I mean, I know this is awkward, but please. My dad's been alone for so long, and I've never seen him happy like this. I hope, I mean, I'd like to know you better. Have you always lived here?"

Alex nodded, and Lucy brightened. "Did you know my mother?"

Ms. LaSalle's mouth dropped open, and my heart stopped. "I... I did," she said.

"Would you tell me about her?" The tone in Lucy's voice was so eager it was almost heartbreaking. "I mean... if that's not weird?"

Ms. LaSalle nodded and blinked down. "What do you want to know?"

"Everything." Lucy made a little laugh.

It was time for me to leave them alone. "I've got to get to the paper office," I said. "Maybe Ms. LaSalle can give you a ride back to Fairview? Or to your house even?"

"Fairview would be fine," Lucy said. "If you don't mind, I mean."

Ms. LaSalle's eyes were shining as she looked at her namesake. "Of course," she said. "We can go back inside."

I watched the two walk up the steps and into the shop before I headed back to my car. Driving back to Fairview, hope filled me and not just for Julian. Maybe this was the start of something bigger—the door to healing slipping open.

Chapter 22

Julian didn't seem to know anything about Lucy's visit with his mom the next day. We went through the entire school routine, business as usual, and no mention of Lucy. I chewed my lip, debating whether to ask him as we walked to our afternoon classes, but he cut through my thoughts.

"I know it's a school night, but could you get away for a little while this evening?" he said, catching my hand. The sly twinkle in his eye made me forget everything but us. "Something's come up, and I want to show you."

"I bet I can steal away for a few minutes." As I leaned forward to kiss him, I wondered if we'd have the house to ourselves. I wondered if we could postpone our deal now that the end of school was rapidly approaching. Who cared who his dad was? We had a major separation looming ahead of us.

"I'll pick you up at your place around eight," he said, kissing me back before he took off for class.

I was left to wonder how I'd make it through the next eight hours.

Waiting for Julian at my house, I couldn't resist sending Lucy a text. I hadn't heard from her last night, and I wondered if she was late with Julian's mom or if they'd gone out to eat. Since Julian hadn't mentioned anything, I was dying to know as I waited for her reply.

Love her!!!!! Lucy replied. *Talked for hours. She loves Dad and told me so much about my mom.*

My brow creased at that. Was it possible Ms. LaSalle would only tell Lucy half of the story? Chewing the inside of my lip I studied my phone before sending a short reply.

Great news! No wicked stepmothers?

Seems v. unlikely, she replied. *More soon!*

After what felt like an eternity, Julian texted that he was in the driveway. It was strange because he always came right in—either to flirt with Mom or through my window; although, it had been a long, sad time since he'd used that tree. Maybe I could suggest we try again. See if we could keep our hands to ourselves. Doubtful.

Dashing down the stairs, I caught a glimpse of my parents on the couch. "Be right back," I called before running through the door.

How I didn't see it coming, I'll never know, but I dashed through the door and froze on the spot. My mouth dropped open, and it was all I could do not to give myself away. Julian was in the driveway, leaning against a polished, steel-grey BMW.

"Well?" He grinned, watching my reaction.

"Oh my god," I gasped, recovering quickly. "But I thought you were getting a truck?"

"Climb in," he said, stepping forward and holding my door. "You're not going to believe how much nicer this rides."

I laughed jumping inside. "I bet it does."

He ran around and climbed in, sitting for a few moments after the car roared to life on the first try. "It's not brand new, but it's new to me!"

"How did you get it?" I was doing my best to be stunned and not smug. Tomorrow I'd be in the Phoenician tower personally thanking his dad. I wanted to hug him for the light in Julian's eyes.

"We'll just go up the road," he said, backing out of the driveway. The car might not've been new, but it smelled new. And the leather interior barely looked used. Of course, Will was the only one driving it, and I wasn't sure how much he even drove in New Orleans.

"If you don't tell me the story…" I said.

He stopped before turning out onto the road and kissed me fast. Then he smiled and kissed me again slower. I was just reaching for his face when he pulled away and turned his attention back to driving. "Mom said she'd been saving up for college. Then when I got the scholarships, she said she wanted to get me a decent car for my regular trips home."

He didn't look at me as he spoke, and I pressed my lips together, unsure if I wanted to pursue it. "Okay," I said, watching him.

But he turned to me quickly. "This is a lot better than decent."

I nodded.

"Whatever," he exhaled, speeding up on the deserted road. "I'm not looking a gift car in the mouth."

Julian's Beemer was the talk of school the next day, and it reminded me of when Brad got his Camaro last fall. Only this time, Julian gave him an immediate "No" when Brad suggested they take it drag racing.

"I told you I've taken my last hit for you," Julian laughed.

Brad slapped him on the back. "You're getting soft," he teased.

Summer was equally impressed, and she was even more adamant about us being Cutest Couple in the yearbook. I was worried she kept saying it in front of everyone until Rachel reminded me she and Brad were up for Mr. and Miss Fairview High School. After that, I was onboard. If only our "couple" status were less frustrating.

Julian and I hadn't done a thing since our agreement about his dad, and when I'd asked him last night if he'd be back, he'd said no. Ms. LaSalle hadn't been spending her nights out lately, he said. I couldn't help wondering if getting caught by Lucy had anything to do with her sudden stay-at-home habits.

Either way, after school, I was in my car headed to the Phoenicians to thank Mr. Kyser and let him know how happy he'd made his son.

Riding up the elevator, I wondered if he knew about Lucy's discovery. And if he did, I wondered if he might be more open to try again with telling Julian the truth. The metal doors opened at the penthouse, and I nearly jumped out of my skin. Will stood in the breezeway waiting, and when he saw me, his face turned into a scowl.

Quickly, he stepped into the elevator and pressed the close button, holding it and preventing my exit.

"What are you doing?" I said, trying to get around him.

He didn't move. "I should say the same to you." His voice was so much like his dad's, but where Mr. Kyser's sternness was all business, Will's felt personally mean. "Why do you keep showing up here? And don't give me any crap about a book."

My eyes flew wide. A book? ...*Summer!* "I told you, I work for the paper," I said trying not to appear flustered, which I knew he would interpret as me lying.

At the same time, anger warred against the intimidation tightening my lungs. Why did he have Summer spying on me? And for that matter, why would she agree to do it? Was that why she'd followed me to the paper office? And what about her nonstop picture-taking? Did Will know something about Julian?

"You used to date my brother," he said. "Did something happen?"

I couldn't look at him without blinking. A little bead of sweat rolled down the center of my back. "No," I said. "I mean, yes, I did, but nothing happened."

He stepped toward me, and I struggled to keep my hands at my sides and not shove him back. "I'm going to find out what's going on, and if something happened, if you're blackmailing Dad, don't think I won't make you regret it."

"You're nuts," I managed to say in a calm voice. "How could I blackmail your dad?"

He stepped back, releasing the close button and allowing me to pass. The metal doors reopened, and I backed out into the penthouse breezeway, holding his gaze the entire time. His cold, blue eyes kept my chest tight, and when the doors finally closed, I let out a deep exhale, almost falling over.

Turning toward the receptionist, I found her desk empty, so I went straight to Mr. Kyser's office. It was also empty.

For a moment, I wondered why Will hadn't said his father wasn't even here. Then my lips pressed together. That was probably why he'd had the nerve to hold me in the elevator. Either way, it didn't matter. What I wanted right now was to locate Summer and get to the bottom of this.

Chapter 23

From the Phoenician penthouse, I drove to the paper office in Fairview. Summer might not be working, but I was going to find out. I couldn't wait another minute to have it out with her. Luckily for me, she was sitting at the makeshift desk, scrolling through picture files. I went straight to her and grabbed the back of the chair, turning it to face me.

"Whoa!" she cried in her dumb, air-head voice. She started to laugh until she saw my face. "Anna?"

"What the hell, Summer?" I shouted, causing Nancy to emerge from her office.

"Is there a problem, girls?" Our editor said, looking from my furious expression to Summer's clueless one.

Suddenly, I wasn't so sure I wanted the Associated Press in on this story. "Sorry," I said, working hard to soften my tone. "I need to talk to Summer about one of our classes." I turned to my ex-friend. "Would you mind if we went outside?"

Nancy's brows pulled together, and I was pretty sure she didn't believe me. But she nodded and went back into her office. Summer stood and followed me out to the courtyard behind our building.

"You want to talk about English?" she said when we got outside. I waited for the door to close completely before continuing.

"I want to know why you're spying on me for Will Kyser."

Her face went from shock to curiosity to a look I'd never seen on Summer, cunning. "He told you?"

This turn of events took me aback. It also made me contemplate my answer. "Let's just say he mentioned the book I lost."

At that, she changed entirely back to airhead. "Oh," she said in that voice I now realized was a cover. "I might've mentioned that you were worried about losing his dad's book."

"Why were you talking to him about me in the first place?"

She turned away, studying her hand. "Umm... I ran into him during Mardi Gras, and I guess I wanted to help you if I could."

"Cut the crap, Summer. I don't believe you for a second," I said, crossing my arms. "You said Casey Simpson is your cousin, right?"

"I don't see the connection." She was back to the high-pitched voice.

"I don't either." I walked around the courtyard, thinking how interested Will was in me and Jack. "But if I catch you spying on me, I'll do something about it." I had no idea what. "And we're not friends anymore."

Her eyes flashed, and that old cunning was back. "We never were," she said. "You pretended to be my friend, but I didn't want to know you. Not after you stole Jack."

"Stole Jack?" I almost laughed out loud. "What the hell?"

"Laugh all you want," she spat. "Like you're so much better than me. He was supposed to be mine after Casey left."

I rubbed my forehead, looking up at the darkening sky. Jack was the least of my concerns. "I don't know what you're talking about," I sighed. "And it's getting late."

"I'm sure you don't know what I'm talking about," she snapped. "You had your head up your ass the entire fall semester. Or I guess I should say his."

My arms dropped, and I went to the glass doors. "I can't argue with that," I said. "I was kind of knocked off my feet by Jack. But I'm back on them now. And you'd better stay out of my way."

I left her standing there, and as I went back to my car, I felt exhausted. All of this intrigue and lying and spying and sudden reveals was starting to wear me down. Why couldn't I just have a normal life, a normal boyfriend, the things you see on the after-school specials. Instead I had Jack, who'd spun my head and then jerked me around. I had Julian, who I loved and couldn't tell the truth about something that was tearing him up inside. And now I had fake friends spying on me and getting me in trouble with crazy older brothers who had hidden agendas.

By the time I made it back home, all I wanted was to sleep. And that's exactly what I did.

Julian could tell something was up as he walked me to class after lunch Friday. "I've missed you a lot these last few days," he said, holding my hand.

I nodded and smiled, squeezing his hand as we walked. The end of the year felt like it was racing toward us, and I wondered where we would be this time next year.

I wasn't encouraged.

"Mom told me she'd be gone tonight," he continued. "That's a pretty big switch, don't you think?"

"Sure," I said. He still didn't seem to know about Lucy's discovery, but I figured since their cat was out of the bag, Ms. LaSalle had to plan her visits now. And since they knew Julian and Lucy were friends, it was smart to be open.

He frowned, studying my face. "Still love me?"

My chest clenched and I stopped walking. He stopped, too, waiting. "How can you ask me that?" I caught his face and kissed him.

That brought out the grin I loved. "Just checking. You've been kind of distant lately. And what's up with you and Summer? I was just getting used to her weirdness."

I shook my head. "She got to be too much. I asked her to give me some space."

He poked out his lips and nodded. "No complaints here."

We started walking again. "So you're saying tonight?"

"Yep," he smiled and kissed the back of my hand. "Can't wait."

"Me either."

The idea of him with me, back in my bed holding me tight in his arms, made everything that was troubling me wash away in a wave of anticipation.

Chapter 24

Mom and Dad of course chose that night to take me out for a celebratory dinner in honor of graduation and my acceptance into Loyola and even better, my scholarship. Mom said the time was racing until graduation, to which I silently agreed. So in honor of the occasion, we drove to Jesse's. I did my best not to think about the last time I was at the tiny upscale restaurant on the Magnolia River.

On that night, Jack had ordered steaks for both of us. I'd had mine with gouda grits. We'd danced, and after, we'd driven down to the beach and made out. It was the night I'd decided to be honest with him. After which, he'd promptly taken me home.

Clearly, I failed at not thinking about the last time I was at Jesse's.

I did not order the steak. I got the New Orleans barbecue shrimp in honor of my future hometown, followed by shrimp and grits. I wasn't going to make the grits suffer because I'd made a poor first choice in boyfriends.

Dinner was actually very nice. Mom and Dad split a bottle of wine. Then they got weepy remembering my first day of kindergarten, and I tried not to roll my eyes. At the end of the evening, I drove us all home nicely bonded and ready for bed. It was late, and I loitered in the kitchen as my parents said goodnight and then went to their rooms. I was confident they'd be sound asleep sooner rather than later.

Once I was certain they were settled, I headed up the stairs. Julian was waiting in my bedroom when I got there, but his appearance stopped me in my tracks. He sat on the floor beside my bed, and when I saw what was in his hands, my stomach fell two stories to the floor below.

He had the letter. And it was clear he'd read it. Even worse, his expression said he was furious. "I've been waiting for you," he said, teeth clenched.

My chest was so painfully tight, it hurt to breathe. "Mom and Dad took me to a surprise dinner." I managed to say, despite the fear climbing my shoulders. "How long have you been here?"

"How did you get this?" he said, holding up the evidence. "It's my mom's handwriting. It's to Bill Kyser. It says he's—"

"Mr. Kyser gave it to me," I jumped in quickly. "But..."

"Why the hell would he give this to *you*?"

The way he said *you* stopped my heart. My eyes grew damp as I crossed the room to him, dropping to my knees at his side. "Oh my god, Julian, it's such a long story. Please let me tell it to you before you think anything..."

But he pushed away. "All I want to know is why you have it. And how long have you had it? How long have you known?"

I hiccupped a breath. "I saw him with your mom. When you were in the hospital last fall. He was comforting her, and it all led to this. But he made me swear never to tell anyone. That's who she's been going to every night. I tried to make them tell you, but they wouldn't. Julian..." my voice cracked as tears blinded my eyes.

"You knew he was my dad all this time, and you didn't tell me?" His voice strained as he said the words, but he was holding himself steady. It completely freaked me out. I could not lose him again. Not for them.

"I wanted to so much." I reached for him, but he blocked my hands. Then he stood up quick. I was right behind him.

"Oh, god, Julian," I cried. "They made me promise not to tell you. Please don't be mad at me."

He only shook his head and was through my window before I could stop him. "Wait!" I tried to catch his arm, but he was going down fast. He made it half-way to the bottom and jumped to the ground, taking off running into the night.

I didn't even think. I grabbed my bag and dashed out my bedroom door, down the stairs and out the door after him. In the distance I heard a car driving off, and I went back inside, scribbled a quick note to my parents, and grabbed the keys to the Civic. I'd never catch a Beemer, but I had to try.

It felt like hours passed with me driving up and down the beach road straining my eyes for any sign of him. The Beemer was back at his mom's house, but after beating on the door and yelling, I gave up. He wasn't there.

Finally, I parked my car at the Romar Beach pavilion and walked out to the water. I didn't know what else to do. My breath caught when I saw a dark figure sitting down by the water. The closer I got, the surer I was.

Fighting against the urge to run and tackle him, I slowly walked to the shoreline. I looked out at the water. I listened to the waves crash. My arms hugged around my waist, and I took a slow breath, thinking about what to say. Coming up with nothing, I turned back to face him.

I sat next to Julian on the sand, and for several long minutes we didn't speak. We only watched the waves crashing, and I thought about all the times I'd studied these waters. At last, he spoke.

"As close as we were and you never told me?" His voice was quiet. "How could you keep that from me?"

I did my best to stay calm. "I kept begging them to tell you. You don't know how many times I almost told you anyway."

He propped his arms on his bent knees and looked down, but I reached out and held his hand.

"Please, Julian," I was trying not to cry, but my voice broke anyway. "Please don't shut me out. I love you."

"Don't go there, Anna." His tone hurt worse than anything.

"It's true," I said, desperation clear in my voice. "And you love me. This has nothing to do with us."

His eyes flashed. "It has a little to do with us. You've been hiding things from me again. How you could go on knowing Jack was my brother and not tell me?"

"I… I promised," I whispered, looking down. "It had nothing to do with him either."

At that, Julian dropped his arms and stood. "I'm going to see him."

My brows pulled together. "Jack?"

"My father." He caught my hand then. "And you're coming with me."

"But—" The look on Julian's face shut my mouth. I nodded. "Let's go."

I followed him back up the long stretch of sand to the parking lot. I knew Julian's car was back at his house.

"Should I drive?" I asked, almost afraid to speak.

"No," he said. "Let's get the new car."

We drove in silence to his mom's house, where we got into the shining Beemer and headed off toward Hammond Island. He didn't look at me the entire time, and my stomach was in knots. I was completely desperate. I would not let his stupid, selfish parents break us up. Not now. Not after all we'd been through. Julian was mine, and they were going to fix this or I'd be figuring out a way to make them.

The drive went by in a blur. The last time I'd driven this way with Julian was the night of Jack and Lucy's birthday party. That night had ended with me running from the house after seeing Jack with Casey Simpson, and Julian chasing after me trying to console me. He'd wanted to take me home, but I'd sent him back inside to be with his half-sister. Neither of us knew about the family connection then, and I wondered if Julian was thinking about it now.

When we arrived at the house, the only car in the driveway was the silver Audi. Lucy wasn't here, but I knew who was. We both knew. He parked the car and walked around to help me out, still silent.

"Julian, wait." I said.

He stopped to look at me, but his expression was closed.

"Before we go in there, just listen to me." He started to turn away, but I grabbed his arm hard. "I'm sorry. I'm sorry I ever knew about this. I never wanted to know this secret, and more than that, I never wanted to keep it from you."

"I appreciate your concern."

"Julian, stop!" I cried. "I've been on your side the whole time, but I had to keep my word. Please believe me. I've been begging them to tell you. And when we go in there now, I'm still on your side. You deserved to know the truth."

Finally he exhaled. His shoulders dropped as he looked down. I held my breath watching his actions until he finally pulled me into his arms. I almost burst into tears. My knees were weak, and my body shook as he stroked my back.

"Calm down," he said. "I don't want to be mad at you. I just want to know the truth."

"Oh, Julian." I reached up to pull his face to mine. He kissed me briefly, but he pulled away, focused on what was coming. I felt only slightly better. He was still angry, and I wasn't entirely out of the woods with him yet. They'd better fix this.

We entered the large home, and Julian walked straight into the living room.

"Mom?" He shouted, looking up and around. "Please come here. I need to speak to you. Mom!"

My eyes were huge, my whole body tense. I heard noises from upstairs. A few seconds passed before Ms. LaSalle appeared on the landing. She was only slightly disheveled, and it seemed she hadn't been here long.

"Julian?" she said, glancing at me. "What's this about?"

"That's what I'd like to know. I was at Anna's and I found this." He pulled out the letter and placed it on the coffee table. His mother quickly descended and picked it up. Just then, Mr. Kyser appeared and began walking down the stairs. He looked resigned, and when he made it to the bottom, he walked over and poured himself a scotch.

"How did you get this?" she said.

"Maybe you should ask my dad." Julian's voice was sharp, and Ms. LaSalle's eyes flashed to me, but he cut her off. "She didn't tell me anything, and I don't like you making Anna lie for you."

Calm permeated her tone. "I didn't mean for her to find out. I never wanted you to know—"

"Why not?" His voice rose. His whole body was tense, and my stomach was sick. "You didn't think I needed to know? You made that choice for me?"

"Julian…" She reached for his arm, but he pulled away.

"Stop it, Mom. You were only thinking of yourself."

"That is not true," she snapped. "I have always thought of you. You've had everything you ever needed, and we've always been fine by ourselves."

"I never had a dad." He looked at Mr. Kyser. "Why did you let her do this?"

His father lowered the scotch glass. "I don't tell your mother what to do, Julian. Whatever she wants is fine with me."

"At least you're honest about it." Julian turned away. I didn't know what to say. Ms. LaSalle stepped forward and touched his arm. Her voice was gentle now, but I could tell it bristled her son. "Julian? Baby? What are you thinking?"

He wouldn't look at her. "I'm not a baby. I haven't been for a long time. And it would've been nice to have a dad."

Mr. Kyser placed his drink down and stepped forward to put his hands on Ms. LaSalle's shoulders. "Julian, please don't be angry with your mother. She was trying to protect you." He exhaled. "I'm not exactly a model father."

Julian looked at him, and his expression made my chest hurt. "You gave up that easily? Didn't you even care?"

"Of course I did." He stepped toward his son. "But… your mother was right. The truth would've only made your life more difficult."

"How?" Julian said.

"It's a small town. I don't exactly have a lot of privacy."

"So you let me go."

"I've always maintained contact."

Julian shook his head. "It's not that easy. You can't just send money and have that make it okay."

Mr. Kyser's hands were open, as if he wanted to reach out. "I know," he said. "You needed more."

"What did you need?" Ms. LaSalle cut in angry. "You had everything. I made sure there was nothing you didn't have."

Julian rubbed his hand over his eyes. "I needed a dad. I needed to know who I was, other than some bastard kid with a hippy mom who lived on the beach like a gypsy. It doesn't instill a lot of confidence."

His mother wouldn't hear any of it. "You have always been confident. Look at you now! Everyone's holding their breaths to see what you'll do next. That other stuff's just in your head."

He pulled away. "You don't understand."

"I understand," Mr. Kyser said. This time he did put his hand on Julian's shoulder. "This doesn't make up for the past, but now you know the truth. I'm glad you know, and I want you to feel like you can come to me for anything."

"Whatever." Julian shook his head. "I don't want a handout from you."

"I don't just mean money. You're an interesting kid, Julian, and I've never regretted being your dad. I wish I could've handled things differently."

"I've got to go." Julian caught my hand. "C'mon, Anna."

"Wait!" His mother stepped toward him.

"No!" I had never seen Julian so angry. "You just stay here. With him."

He turned and stalked out, me right behind him.

"Give him some space." I heard Mr. Kyser saying as we left the house.

When we got to the car, Julian stopped. I waited facing him until he reached forward and wrapped his arms around my shoulders, pulling me to him. I held his waist tightly, and I could feel him trembling.

"Are you okay?" I asked softly.

He nodded.

"What do you want to do?" I said, still holding him.

His voice was thick. "I don't know."

"Are you mad at me?"

He kissed my head, squeezing me again. "No. Those two can be pretty intimidating."

I squeezed him and stepped back to see his face. "I love you."

He nodded then glanced up at me. "Where does that leave my brother?"

My nose wrinkled. "That's kind-of weird, huh?"

"Not as weird as Lucy being my sister. Jesus, that was close. And dammit! They knew the whole time."

"I'm not defending them," I started cautiously. "But they were concerned about that. Part of what they were talking about when I found them in the hospital was separating you two without blowing their cover."

He exhaled and leaned against the car. "Why wouldn't they tell me?"

I leaned beside him. "They've got a long story and pretty good reasons," I said, wondering if they would tell him everything. "And I think your mom worried the truth might change you."

"I'm glad she's got so much confidence in me." He stood and helped me into the car. "I don't know. Maybe she's right. Maybe if I'd known, I wouldn't have worked so hard. Maybe I'd have ended up as lost as Lucy."

He got in and turned us out of the flagstone drive onto the road.

"She's not so lost now," I said. "And at least your mom adores you. Mr. Kyser completely shut Lucy out."

"I guess he can be a real jerk." Then Julian shook his head. "I don't know. That's just what I've heard."

"Maybe you should get to know him for yourself." I was trying to tread lightly. "He loves your mom a lot, and maybe... it would've been different if they'd gotten together."

We drove in silence a few minutes. Then he exhaled with a tight smile.

"What?" I asked.

"I guess I should've thanked him for this car."

"Oh. Yeah."

We were quiet again, and I decided not to tell him my role in the whole car-buying decision. I didn't want to risk him getting mad at me again. Our fingers were entwined, and he turned mine over to look at my ring. Then he reached up and stroked my cheek.

"I guess I know who my dad is now," he said. "And you're wearing my ring."

In spite of it all, a little thrill tingled in my stomach. "That was the deal." My voice sounded shaky. My insides were a blend of relief he wasn't angry, happiness we were together, and excited nervousness about what he was suggesting.

"I'm sorry I blamed you." His voice was slowly returning to that familiar cocky playfulness I knew and loved. "Maybe you could come back to my house. We could kiss and make up?"

My heart jumped. "Sure."

Chapter 25

We drove back to the small cottage on Crystal Shores Boulevard. It was dark, and he led me inside to his bedroom. I looked around. I'd been to Julian's house a million times, but we'd always stayed in the garage where he worked. I'd never actually been back here. Sketch books were scattered around, and I walked over and opened the cover of one lying on the desk. It had figure drawings that I recognized as a few of his larger sculptures. A popping noise from the other room distracted me, and soon he was back handing me a bubbling glass.

"I've kind of given up alcohol for the duration—" I started.

"I know, but it might relax things."

"Oh." I nodded feeing a flush. "Right."

I turned back to the book, carefully flipping the pages to a few sketches that looked familiar. "Is this me?" I asked, pointing in the book.

He leaned over and smiled. "Yeah. I'd get bored and start thinking about you."

His words made me feel fizzy, and I took a big gulp, setting an empty glass on the side table.

He laughed. "Don't chug it. I'd like you to be conscious."

Then he pulled me to him, kissing me gently on the mouth. Heat radiated through my stomach, and I wished I'd taken another drink. I still felt nervous.

"Are you okay?" he asked softly.

I nodded and burped. We both laughed.

Julian slipped off his shirt, and I lightly ran my finger down his chest to the round tattoo, where I spread my palm flat. He pulled me to him and gave me a kiss before lifting my shirt over my head. I quickly removed my bra and reached around his waist to pull our bodies together. His hands slid down my bare back, and I shivered.

"Cold?" he whispered kissing my shoulder.

"A little," I whispered back.

He led me to his bed and lifted the covers for me to climb in. I slid under them as he unfastened his pants and slipped them off. For a second I admired the lines on his chest leading down past the ink on his side, down the center of his stomach, all the way to...

He quickly slipped in next to me and pulled me under him, covering my mouth with his. Every part of my body was hot, but my nervousness subsided as he kissed a trail from my neck down to my chest, pausing to run his tongue around my most sensitive parts. A little sound came from my throat. I was acutely aware of all his touches. His hands unfastened my jeans, and I quickly helped him take them off along with my panties. I'd never been completely naked with him before, and it was thrilling.

He leaned away for a second, reaching inside his drawer. I saw the square packet and understood what he was doing when I heard the rip. Then he was back. His lips closed on mine again, my body was pulsing inside and out.

"I'm going to try and make it not hurt so much," he whispered.

I didn't know what he meant, but he was gone again. And the next thing I felt were light kisses on the inside of my thigh. He pushed my legs apart and my heart leaped as his lips moved higher. When his tongue lightly touched me, a burst of pleasure shot through my entire body. I could feel a building sensation below my waist. A few seconds more, and I was gripping the sheets.

Everything changed in an instant. Pleasure rocketed through me, shuddering my limbs, and as soon as it happened Julian was back, pushing inside me.

It did hurt, like ripping a scab off before it's ready, but my body was still trembling from the intense high I'd just reached. It wasn't as bad as I'd expected, and he slowly began pushing harder. The pain grew more intense, and I bit my lip to keep from making a sound. I had to get through this. He kept moving, and I could tell he was doing his best to be gentle. I felt a shudder pass through him as if he were struggling with restraint.

I tried to adjust my position, rotate my hips, find a way to help him, but he gasped a noise in my ear each time I moved. His pace increased, and my eyes closed. I held him a few more seconds, and a low groan came from his throat. He held me tightly for a bit more, then he relaxed. I wrapped my arms around him and we held each other as our hearts beat together, our breath equally fast.

His body was less tense as he moved to lie beside me. "Are you okay?" he whispered.

I nodded.

"Hurt too much?"

I looked down. I didn't want him to feel bad. He quickly rose on his side and looked into my eyes, and I rolled on my side away from him. I didn't want him to see me cry.

"Anna?" He put his hand on my shoulder.

I couldn't stop the tears then, but I didn't really

know why I was crying. It hadn't hurt that bad. Not bad enough to cry. Julian pulled me onto my back, but I rolled my face into his chest.

"What's wrong?" he asked softly.

"I don't know," I sniffed. "I just… it hurt, and I don't know. I thought… maybe it wouldn't."

"What?"

"I just… I love you, and it was you and me, and I just thought…"

"That I'd be freakishly small or something?"

"No…" I started to giggle through my tears. "You are *not* small."

"Thanks."

My hand shot forward into his stomach. He grunted a laugh, and then we both started laughing. "You set me up for that."

He laughed again and rubbed my back. I slid my arm around his waist, tears forgotten.

"I'm sorry I hurt you," he said, kissing my shoulder. "I was hoping it might be less painful if you… you know. Went first."

"That was amazing," I lifted my chin to look at him.

He smiled. "It gets better. I promise." He kissed the tear off my cheek.

"Really? Because up to the end, it was really great."

Just then I felt a trickle between my legs.

"Oh! Let me out!"

He stood up quickly, and I raced to the bathroom. I jumped on the toilet, but I was afraid I'd waited too long. It only took a few wipes for the bleeding to stop, but then I realized I was stuck in the bathroom with no clothes. I looked around, on the shower door, under the cabinet, but all I could find was a hand towel on the sink. *What was this? Laundry day?*

I grabbed it and held it in front of me as I walked back to Julian's room. The small towel only covered my lower half, and when he saw me, he grinned.

"Um… you missed a spot." The approval in his voice made my stomach tighten.

"Close your eyes," I whispered.

"No way," he said, propping on his elbow. "You're beautiful."

My arms readjusted so I could cover my breasts. "You're embarrassing me."

"Why? It's the truth." He sat all the way up and pulled me to him, moving my arm. "Maybe I could sketch you like this." He kissed my ribs, working his way higher, as my breath caught.

"Right," I gasped, sliding my fingers into his soft hair. "And someone would find it, and I'd die."

"I wouldn't let anyone find it." He pulled me back into the bed, and I wrapped my arms around his neck, our chests pressing together in that luscious way.

"I'm sorry," I whispered. "I think I might've messed up your sheets."

"Don't worry about it." His lips pressed to mine briefly. "I'll take care of it."

He was kissing me slowly, as if he were taking little tastes. I couldn't believe I was warming up again, but I was.

"Do you think it'll hurt again?" I asked.

The edge in his voice only fanned my growing flames. "Want to find out?"

I nodded and he kissed me long and deep as his hands slowly moved down my body. Somehow I got the feeling this would never feel anything but fantastic, ever again.

Light was streaming through the window when I opened my eyes. Julian was asleep beside me with his arm across my waist. I didn't know what time we'd fallen asleep, but the biggest problem was it was morning and I wasn't at home. I sat up fast.

"Julian! Wake up!" He stirred groggily and pulled me back down to him. I struggled to get out of his arms. "Wake up, Julian. My mom's going to freak out if I'm not home."

His voice was a sleepy complaint. "Didn't you leave a note?"

"Yes, but it said I was with you and I'd be back soon. What do you think she'll think if I'm not back and it's morning?"

"We'll make something up. Stop squirming!" He kissed my neck as his arms tightened around my waist.

"Julian! I've got to get home." I tried pushing him off me but he was too heavy, and I couldn't help laughing.

"See?" he said, continuing his trail of kisses. "You don't want to leave me."

I held his neck and kissed him back. "I don't, but I have to get home. They might still be sleeping." His lips were weakening my resolve, but I had to be strong. "If they think we're up to something, they'll make it harder for us to see each other."

"In that case..." He let me go instantly and sat up, grabbing his jeans from the floor and jerking them on. I reached under the covers to find my panties. My jeans were on the floor, too. I pulled them on and my shirt.

"Maybe we could say I had to spend the night because your mom was sick," I said, thinking.

"No good. Why was she sick? And what if your mom offered to bring her food or something?"

I nodded, poking my lips out. "You're right. Why did I leave the house with you?"

He stopped moving and stood straight, seeming to consider this. "Well, I'd just found out Mr. Kyser was really my dad, and I freaked. You left to comfort me, and I ended up deflowering you. Several times."

A charge raced to my toes. "Julian! Get serious."

He laughed. "C'mon. Let's see if they're even awake. Then we'll figure something out. Your mom likes me, remember?"

"I wouldn't press my luck if I were you," I breathed, dashing through the house.

It was before nine when we reached my house, and shockingly no one seemed to be awake.

At the door, I turned back to him. "You'd better go. I'll call you later."

He pulled me in for another long kiss. I slipped my fingers into his hair, thinking how fantastic and wonderful and *special* we were together. He straightened up and looked into my eyes. "I love you."

My stomach flooded with butterflies. "I love you."

He smiled and slipped out the door as I turned back to face… an unbelievably quiet house. I couldn't believe I'd managed to get in and out without notice, but just then I heard my dad coming down the stairs and panicked.

"Anna?" Dad's brow furrowed. "You up already? And dressed? What's going on, honey?"

"Uh… Dad?" My voice was too high. I cleared it. The only story in my head was Julian's deflowering one, and I couldn't tell him that. "Well, I was here and then… I uh…"

He kept walking into the kitchen and stopped at the counter. "We're out of coffee?"

God in heaven. "Yes! And I thought it would be a good idea if I went and got some, but I forgot my purse."

"What's this? A note for Mom?"

"Oh, yeah," I quickly grabbed it off the bar and crumpled it into a ball. "I thought she might get up and wonder where I was. So I'll be back in five, and we can all have some coffee. Want me to get a go-cup for you?"

"That's okay, I can wait." Then he grinned. "I'll just crawl back in bed with Mom."

"Right. Well, nobody wants to hear about that!"

"Ah, grow up, Anna."

"Bye, now!"

I ducked out the front door and leaned against the wall of the carport for a half second, exhaling as my heart rate slowed back to normal. Last night had been too crazy even for me, and that was just beyond close.

Chapter 26

It seemed all of Fairview was in the drive-through waiting for coffee, but I didn't want to go inside. Sitting in my car, the realization washed over me: I was free. The Secret was out. The letter was back with Mr. Kyser, Julian had confronted both his parents, and best of all, he wasn't mad at me. Far from it.

With a happy flush, I remembered his hands on my body, his lips. Then I remembered *my* hands on his body and his reaction. Leaning forward, I placed my forehead on the steering wheel and closed my eyes. At one point in the night he'd held my face in both his hands, looked deep into my eyes, and told me he loved me. My stomach did a little flip again.

Grabbing my phone, I had to call one person immediately.

"An-nAH!" Gabi's voice sang out.

I held the phone away from my ear and winced. "Did you just sing my name?"

"Sidney and I are working on a video in which I am the diva Lady G."

"I don't even know which question to ask first," I laughed. "Is this for school or funniest home videos?"

"Neither, and you can hold your applause to the end."

"That might be a long hold," I snorted. "Gabi. You don't sing."

"Off the record," her voice was overly dramatic, "I'm lip-syncing, but it's my scandalous secret. Don't tell. It would ruin my career if it came out."

"It's in the vault." I leaned out the window and ordered a pound of coffee to go as my best friend continued.

"Seriously, what's up?" she asked. "I haven't heard from you in a month."

I took a deep breath and told her. "I did it."

"Did what?"

"It."

"Holy shit!" she screamed. "Was it Julian?"

"Of course."

"Was it great?"

I giggled. "Of course."

"Oh my god! Details, details!"

"Well, first, the whole thing about his parents came out." I quickly gave her the rehash. "We left Hammond Island, and it's still not clear how that'll play out. He is really mad at his mom—"

"And then he was all, 'Let's get it ooon'?" she interrupted.

"Please stop singing," I groaned. "But yes. Then it happened."

We both were quiet for a moment. "Okay," Gabi said. "So what now?"

"I don't know." I was at the window, and the barista gave me a disapproving look. I mouthed a *sorry* and took my bag. "But he was *so* sweet to me, and after that first time—"

"You did it more than once!" Gabi screamed again.

"Oh, well…" My face felt hot. "I really love him," I said quietly. "And after that first time I was so disappointed and he was so affectionate. We kind of fell asleep, but we woke up later and that's when it really got good."

"Julian is so hot," she sighed. "And you've got what? Like a month or so before you leave for college?"

"Oh…" Everything changed with her words. I knew it was there, I knew the facts, but somehow hearing it, knowing we were so close, my eyes flooded. "Oh, god…"

"Anna?" Gabi's voice was worried. "Are you okay?"

"I don't know." Blinking hard, I had to pull over. I couldn't see for the tears that wouldn't stop coming. "Oh, Gabi." My body shook so hard, I had to put my head on the steering wheel again. "He can't leave me."

"Wait… But you're leaving, too." Her voice was softer, and it only made the pain worse. The miles seemed to stretch out between us, and it was all coming so fast. It was why I'd hidden the scholarship letter, why I didn't want to tell him. And now this.

"Anna?" I could hear the panic in her voice.

"I'm here," I whispered.

"Oh, thank goodness. Now come on, breathe. What did Julian say about it?"

"He said…" I shook my head. "He said we'd talk about it when the time came. But what if he says we should break up—"

"He's *not* going to say that." Gabi's voice was stern. "Julian would never break up with you now."

My stomach twisted with burning knots at her words. "Maybe I could go with him?" My mind was moving fast. "He said something about me being in Savannah and how great that would be."

"If you didn't have your own plans," she argued. "And if you hadn't gotten the queen of all nerds scholarship!"

"I don't care!" I was breathless, frantic.

"Holy crap, Anna! You are not throwing away a full ride to a top school for a guy."

I knew she was right, I knew it. At the same time... "But it's Julian!"

"He won't let you do it either," she continued. "I'm calling your mom."

I closed my eyes for a second, trying to calm down. My heart was pounding, but I managed to slow my breathing. "Gabi, I love him."

"I know," she said, her voice gentler. "So let's think about it."

I thought too quickly. "It's at least 600 miles from New Orleans to Savannah." The tears were back. "It'll never work out."

"Why don't you talk to him about it? I bet you two could do like a meet in the middle deal or go home on the weekends. That's actually a longer drive for him."

"Sorry, Gab, I gotta go."

"Are you going to be okay?"

"I don't know, but I'll call you," I said, hitting end. It felt like a lead weight was pressing on my chest.

Everything was different now, and the thought of us being separated was impossible to even imagine. I needed to see him. I needed to spend every waking second with him—every night too, for that matter. Dad was waiting on coffee, but I turned the car south toward the beach.

Julian was in his garage when I arrived, but instead lifting heavy metal, he was standing behind a canvass holding a brush. The sight of him made my insides swell with joy in spite of our miserable future. I was so in love with him. His blue eyes caught me, and he stood quickly, stowing the brush on his easel.

"Hey," he said, jogging over. "What are you doing here? I didn't think I'd see you until at least this evening."

I stepped forward, pushing my arms around his waist and my head to his chest. "I needed to see you," I said, fighting tears. "I talked to Gabi."

He took my hands and led me to the bench near the door. "Is something wrong?"

We were facing each other now, my leg bent in front of us, and his brows were pulled together over his bright eyes.

"I hope you don't mind if I told her about us," I said.

His faced relaxed into that teasing grin. "Did you tell her I was the king and all that good stuff?"

I closed my eyes, looking down. "I didn't go into details. But, Julian…" Then my eyes blinked back to his, worried. "What happens now? What are we going to do?"

He was still grinning. "Hopefully a lot more of what we did last night."

"I'm serious. We're going to be a million miles apart come August."

That removed his grin. He scooted forward and pulled me into a hug, which made my eyes flood again. His arms were around me, and my face was pressed into his shoulder. I inhaled his warm scent of sunshine and ocean and soap, until a hiccupped breath jerked my body.

"Hey," he leaned back, catching my cheeks in his hands. "Don't do that."

For a moment, I could only study his handsome face. Dark hair messy, blue eyes. Savannah seemed like my only choice. I blinked and two tears hit my cheeks.

His brow creased, and he wiped them away with his thumbs. "Stop," he whispered. "We've got months until August."

I shook my head. "It's only going to get worse, and by then it'll be unbearable." My voice cracked as I spoke. "Why didn't I apply to Savannah?"

"Because you didn't want to go there? Because we weren't together. It doesn't matter now."

"It does. I can't even think about us being separated like that."

"So don't," he shrugged, dropping his hands. "It'll just ruin the time we have now. When August gets here, we'll deal with it."

"I don't know how I'll deal with it," I dropped my head, but he caught my chin.

"We will." His blue eyes were firm, and I inhaled a shaky breath. My lips pressed together, and I tried to believe him. I had to believe him. I didn't have a choice.

"But what about the separation?" I said, my voice the slightest bit stronger.

He shrugged, pulling me into his chest. "It'll suck," he exhaled. "But we had a little time last month to practice."

"Oh, god, and it was awful."

"I say we stockpile being together." He kissed the top of my head, and I could hear the smile in his voice. "What better way to prepare?"

His tone made me smile. The tiniest flicker of hope stirred in my chest, and I held his arms. "I'm willing to try anything."

"That's my girl," he squeezed, then pushed me back up to face him. The determined look was still in his eyes, and thinking of all the ways he'd proven his love in the last year fanned that flicker of hope into something bigger. Maybe it was possible. If he'd inherited even half the stubbornness of his parents, he could make anything happen.

"We're not breaking up," he said. "We're not saying goodbye. We'll focus on finishing school, and take every opportunity to be together."

"It's a really long drive," I said, thinking. "Good thing you've got that nice car now."

His smile grew bigger. "So I'm doing all the driving?"

"Of course not. But you'll be lucky if I go back to New Orleans if I do," I teased, catching his hand and lacing our fingers. "What are you working on over here?"

He pulled back, stopping me. "Nope. You can't see it."

My eyes narrowed, and I took a quick step toward the back of the garage. He caught me around the waist, easily lifting me and carrying me away. "Julian!" I squealed.

"It's something special." His mouth was at my ear, and a little charge tingled down my neck. I wasn't sure if he noticed, but when he put me down, his voice was lower. "We should go inside and get started on that stockpile."

My insides warmed, and I hugged my arms around his neck. "Can't," I said, kissing him quickly. "Dad's going to kill me. I never made it back with his coffee."

"Why did you run off with your dad's coffee?"

"I had to buy more, but I sort-of wigged in the coffee line." I took off out the door back to my car. Julian followed me, and when I stopped, he gave me a kiss.

"It's going to work out," he said, looking straight into my eyes.

"I believe you," I said, kissing him back before jumping in the car and heading to my house.

Chapter 27

My phone startled me awake, and the first thing I noticed was Julian was gone. I sighed, running my hand over the now-cool spot in my bed that had become his almost-constant nighttime location. He'd decided our code word was *shortage*, and it was silly enough that I'd agreed. Now "shortage" was my all-time favorite problem to hear.

Lifting my phone, I expected to see his face, and I sat straight up when I didn't. The number staring back at me was one I hadn't seen on my phone since New Year's Eve. It was Bill Kyser's.

My voice had the smallest tremor as I answered. "Hello?"

"I'm sorry if I woke you," Julian's dad said, and he actually sounded uncomfortable, too.

"I was awake," I lied quickly. "Did you need something? Well, I mean, of course you did…"

"Anna," he thankfully stopped my rambling. "I'm calling about Julian. It's been a while since I've seen you, and—"

"I never got to thank you for the car!" I said fast.

He paused, then he seemed to remember. "Oh, that was nothing. Just a matter of finding something new for Will and signing his old car over to Alex. That's not why I'm calling."

"Sorry," I said growing quiet.

He took a deep breath before continuing. "Julian hasn't been staying at home."

My face flushed, and I didn't know what to say to that. Did he know Julian spent most nights here?

It didn't seem to matter.

"Alex is upset. She wants to talk to him, but he won't speak to her."

I chewed my lip, thinking. I knew Julian was pissed at his mom, but I didn't know they weren't speaking. "I'm sorry about that," I said. "With school ending and everything, I've kind of been distracted. But what—"

"I'd like to talk to him. Could you ask him to see me?"

"Me?" My forehead lined. "Why don't you ask him yourself?"

"If he's anything like his father, he'll do whatever you want him to do."

A little charge moved through my stomach at the implication. "What are you going to say to him? If he trusts me, I'm not setting him up for an ambush."

"I wouldn't ambush him," he said. "I just need to know what he's thinking. What his plans are."

"Did Ms. LaSalle ask you to call me?" He didn't answer, and I realized she had. Bill Kyser would never have called me. It all made sense now. "I guess we'll see how much he's like his dad."

"He can visit my office any evening. Text me when he's coming."

Standing in front of the Phoenician I tower holding hands, we both looked up, up, up to the top where his dad's offices were located.

"He didn't say what he wanted?" Julian asked, and I couldn't tell if he was nervous or not. He didn't seem to be.

"Just that your mom's upset, and he wanted to know what you were thinking."

Julian nodded. "She put him up to this."

"And he put me up to this." I turned to face him. "Do you want me there? I don't mind waiting down here for you if you want to be alone."

For a moment, we both thought about it. Then Julian leaned forward and quickly pressed his lips to mine. "Wait for me," he said. "I won't be long, and I can use you as an excuse if things get weird."

"Thanks," I teased. Actually, I was happy to let him use me as his excuse. I felt solely responsible for his being here now.

He disappeared into the high-rise, and I walked down to sit on the shore and wait for him. A steady stream of foot traffic moved past me. It was almost May, and senior trips had started along with families taking their last beach vacations before the whole town blew up for the summer. As for us, only prom and one week of classes remained before graduation.

Julian's unwavering assurance that we would survive the transition and temporary separation helped ease my fears about August, but I could only imagine his mom was a hundred times more worried. I looked down, sliding my sparkling dragonfly ring around on my finger. It had come to symbolize so much more to us than his thanks for my little news story so long ago. Now it was a promise. And I never took it off.

My thoughts were miles away, years into the future, when I noticed a person was standing beside me. Squinting up, I saw Ms. LaSalle looking out at the ocean. She didn't say anything for several moments, then she sat beside me.

"They're all going to react this way," she said. "Julian knows. We have to tell the others, and it's always going to come back to what I did."

Her eyes were tired, and I scooted around on the sand to face her. "You've spent a lot of time with Lucy," I said. "She loves you already. And she's loved getting to know you."

Julian's mom shook her head. "And when she hears the rest of the story, she'll hate me."

My lips pressed together, and my chest felt heavy. "You'd be surprised how understanding Lucy can be. She's been through a lot."

"She won't be able to forgive me for taking away her mother. For being the reason she died." Then she glanced at me. "Bill said he'd given you the journals to read. I can't believe he did that. I can't believe he even had them."

"I couldn't believe he gave them to me either," I said, studying my hands as I thought about my words. "But I'm glad he did. I feel like I understand everything, and reading them... I don't hate you."

Her forehead was lined when she looked at me then, and I saw a glisten in her eyes. "We were so young," she said in a voice that made my throat hurt. "We made such foolish mistakes."

"But you loved each other," I said, reaching for her hand. "You still love each other. And... I can't imagine my life without Julian."

She sniffed and nodded. "He was the one good thing to come of it all." Then she exhaled. "And now he won't even speak to me."

We were still holding hands, and I chewed my lip as I chose my words. "It wasn't fair not letting him know his dad," I said softly. "But at the same time... I understand why you did it. I understand your fears."

"Bill wants to tell them all. He wants to invite everyone home and have us all there together." She looked back at the water. "I'm not sure I'll make it through something like that."

"He won't do it if you're not willing," I said softly, remembering my telephone conversation with him. The reason Julian was in his office now.

"No, he won't," she said softly. "But he wants Julian in his life, and that means telling the others Julian's his son. And that means telling them about me."

For several moments we sat listening to the waves crashing as the wind pushed against us. The waves never stopped. They raged in and swept back out, year after year, regardless of the events impacting the humans on shore.

"I think telling them can wait," I said finally. "At least for a little while. Once college starts, you can decide how you want to handle it. Maybe you could tell Lucy yourself."

Julian's mom continued staring out at the horizon. Then as if waking from a spell, she stood and dusted her skirt. "I'll think about it." Her eyes flitted behind me, and she turned quickly, walking away from me down the shoreline in the direction of her house.

I looked back over my shoulder to see Julian headed in my direction, an angry expression in his eyes.

"Hey!" I jumped up and hurried to meet him. "How'd it go?"

"What was she doing here?"

I hugged his waist, reaching up with a finger to smooth the angry lines off his forehead. "Worrying about you," I said. "I know you're mad, but you're going to have to forgive her some day."

His eyes were still focused on the direction his mother had gone, but then he blinked down to me. I smiled at him, gorgeous even angry, with the wind pushing his dark hair around his head. He returned my smile, softening.

"So?" I laced our fingers and started walking along the shore. "What did he say?"

"At first not much," Julian said, looking out at the water. "We don't really know each other very well. Or at all, I guess."

"You'll get to know each other," I said, squeezing his hand.

He pulled me closer and kissed my head. "He wants me to talk to Mom. It's so weird hearing a man say that to me. 'Talk to your mother, Julian.'"

He imitated Mr. Kyser's voice, and I breathed a laugh at how much they sounded alike. It was crazy. "You've never had a dad bossing you around. Sure you want that?"

We walked a little ways, him contemplating the path ahead of us. "It's not like that. I don't think he wants to boss me around. I kind of… like him."

"He's always loved you," I said, then I realized Julian wasn't aware just how much I knew about his history. "I mean, every time I've talked to him, you're all he wants to know about."

He took my hand again as we walked. "So you found out about this when I was in that wreck?"

I nodded. "He was at the hospital to see you. Well, to check on your mom. I accidentally caught them together."

"I can't believe it. All this time, and I never knew they were together."

"They weren't," I said. "I mean, that's how I got mixed up in it. They weren't together, and they were afraid I'd tell you."

His eyes cut to mine, and I saw that flash of impatience.

"I begged them to tell you," I said quickly. "And I do think that's when they started getting back together."

Again we walked in silence. Finally, Julian stopped and faced the Gulf. I pulled up short beside him. "I've got so many questions. There's so much I want to know."

"I can believe it."

"He was at the hospital that night?"

I nodded, and my chest warmed at his expression.

"Your dad really loves you," I said, slipping my arms around his waist. "You've always been so important to him."

His arms went around me, and I felt his chin rest on the top of my head. For several moments we didn't move, and I could sense something was changing in him. The tension and anger was fading. He was even standing straighter.

"I guess this means I'm somebody," he said.

I pulled back to face him. "You've always been somebody! And it's only going to get better."

He pulled me closer. "Tell me the truth. Do you just love me for my money?"

I laughed. "Of course!" Then he tickled me and I screamed.

We both dropped to sitting on the sand, me in his lap. My arms were around his neck, and his hands held my waist.

"Julian LaSalle, I've loved you since I wouldn't look at you in algebra class," I said softly.

He leaned closer, and I kissed him.

"I wanted to die every time you said something to me," I continued, hugging him tightly.

"That's why I hid behind my books. I've been crazy in love with you for years."

He laughed and shook his head. "Life is so screwed up."

"But somehow it all seems to work out."

Chapter 28

Our prom's theme was "A Night to Remember." I felt like I'd been having nights to remember for months—even more in the last few weeks—so it was perfect for me. Mom was crying and taking too many pictures as we tried to leave my house, and Julian stood around with his hands shoved in his tuxedo pants pockets, seeming uncomfortable with all the emotional display.

My dress was Tiffany blue and strapless. The color made my eyes bright green, and the skirt was filmy chiffon, which made me feel like a mermaid. It was the same length as those cheerleader uniforms Julian always admired, so he was an instant fan. He looked like a rock star in his tux, escorting me to his waiting BMW.

"A night to remember," he said under his breath, holding my door. "We'll have to see if we can live up to that."

I kissed his nose before getting in. "We already have."

"That dress is causing a shortage," he teased.

"I was going to say just the opposite. Something's on the rise..." I winked getting into the car.

He caught me, holding me against the car. "Girl, your mom's already crying. Hearing you talk that way would only make it worse."

I pressed my mouth to his in response, tongues entwining as his fingers tickled at my hem. "Get in before we don't go," he said in a tone that melted my insides.

"A night to remember."

As we drove south toward the Phoenician VI, where the event was taking place, I stared out into the black night. "Did you see your mom before you left?"

He shook his head, and I chewed my lip. Prom was pretty important to parents, and I hated that he was still not speaking to her. I decided to let it go for now and hoped I could find a way to get them back together before August.

Twinkle lights, fake columns, and arbors draped with white tulle filled the ballroom of the enormous high-rise. It was the same venue Brad's dad had donated for the party after our winning basketball game, and the Tiki theme only occasionally peeked out as we made our way through the crowd.

Party photographers snapped pictures nonstop, and Julian and I were frequent subjects as we'd actually managed to land the Cutest Couple title. It seemed our classmates had taken Summer's ruse and run with it. And despite our animosity, she was probably happy. My couple status with Julian solidified her "Jack is mine" position.

The tiniest twinge plucked at my stomach knowing how much I'd see Jack next year. Living with Rachel, with Brad at Tulane, we'd most likely cross paths at least a few times. My reaction to seeing him at the game wasn't encouraging, but I'd cross that bridge when it appeared. I gave Julian's arm a squeeze. I had no doubt who owned my heart now.

Summer circled the room on Blake's arm, and I didn't tell Julian why I preferred to stay with Rachel and Brad while he chatted with his shop buddy. I wasn't about to tell him about her spying or Will's intimidation tactics. As far as I was concerned, I was out of the Kyser family business. I couldn't imagine Will's reaction to meeting Julian, or Jack's for that matter. It was possible I'd be there to witness those introductions with the way things were going, but tonight was not about Kyser family troubles.

"Where are you?" Julian said in my ear, holding me close for a slow dance. His hands were at my waist, and mine were clasped behind his neck. A touch of spice accented his usual beachy scent.

I smiled. "Right where I want to be."

That response earned me a kiss, and we swayed to the music for a while. The dance portion of prom was pretty low-key, and after, we took group photos, avoided Blake and Summer — at least I did — until at last, Julian escorted me to the door, pausing before we exited behind giddy classmates.

"Would you be disappointed if we went back to my house instead of heading to the after-party?" he asked. "I've got something I want to show you."

My brow lined. Brad had built another bonfire on the beach, and everyone was talking about who would be there and what they were bringing. I did want to join them, but he had me curious. "It had better not be a shortage of melons or whatever."

"Melons and bananas?"

My eyes narrowed. "Julian…"

He laughed, "You started it." Our fingers were laced as he led me out to the car. "I'm pretty sure there will be a shortage, but that's not what I want to show you."

I shrugged, "I'm curious."

"Good," he grinned.

The garage workshop at Julian's house was unusually clean, and I noticed candles situated in a few of the windows. A soft yellow light replaced his usual harsh fluorescent bulbs, and the easel he'd been hiding behind the day I'd surprised him was draped with a sheet.

"What's going on?" I asked softly. The whole setup made me feel like I should whisper. It was warm and clearly planned. Any disappointment I felt about skipping the after-party disappeared.

"Mom's spending the night at Dad's..." he paused, blinking as his brows pulled together. Then he did a little laugh. "That's the first time I've said that."

"Does it make you happy?" I caught him around the waist, hugging us close.

He shrugged. "I guess." He rubbed my upper arms, looking down. "It feels like the circle's whole now. Like before it was broken or a segment was missing, and now it's joined. Does that make sense?"

"Yes," I said, then I leaned forward and caught his eyes. "Are you still mad at her?"

Without a word he let me go, stepping to a mini-fridge hidden in the corner. I watched as he pulled out a bottle of sparkling wine and fiddled with the cork.

"Julian?"

He didn't answer, instead he popped open the bottle and poured us both small servings in clear plastic cups. Walking back to me, he finally answered. "Yes."

My lips pressed together. I took my glass from him, unsure how to proceed. His feelings were justified, and I didn't want to spoil our night. Still, I had to know. "Will you ever forgive her?"

Again, he didn't speak right away. I watched as he considered his answer. "Yes," he said again, and I exhaled with relief. He caught me around the waist, pulling me close. "When I think about it all, I get really angry, and I don't want to talk to her." My hand traveled up to his collar, sliding the now-open fabric between my fingers as I listened. "But I know eventually I'll forgive her. I see it happening."

"I understand," I said, smoothing his white shirt-front.

"It just really burns that she lied to me that way. For so long."

My eyes blinked as I thought of the journals, of his dad and how he'd responded to lies. "You get that honest."

"Anyway, let's not talk about it. I want you to see my surprise. Come here."

He took my hand and led me around to the easel sitting in the back corner. "Close your eyes." I did, and a faint swishing followed by movement sounded in front of me. Then he touched my arm. "Open them."

A gasp slipped through my lips. It was a brilliant watercolor painting. "You did this?" I whispered, lightly touching the canvass.

He stepped behind me and wrapped his arms around my waist, resting his chin on my shoulder as I studied it.

In almost transparent layers of color, he'd created a scene of a girl in the bottom left corner. Her light-brown hair was in spirals and she was surrounded by deep purples, greens, and golds with street lamps and wrought iron. Her hand stretched up toward the opposite corner, where a dark-haired boy was leaning back on what looked like a beach. He was surrounded by brown and blue and the corresponding gold, and his hand extended down to hers. Between them both flew a small dragonfly.

Mist clouded my eyes, and I reached for his hand, sliding my finger across the small tattoo near his thumb. Our two little insects appeared to be flying to meet each other at this angle.

"I was thinking about next year and the following years," he said, "and how we'll always have these little guys reminding us."

Tears were in my eyes as I leaned my head back against his chest. He kissed it.

"It's true," I whispered. "Are you giving this to me?"

He laughed softly. "I don't know. I kind of want to keep it for myself to remember. It's going to be hard."

The hoarseness in his voice increased my tears, and I turned to face him. "But you said we'd be okay. We'll make it work, right?"

He smiled and bent down to kiss me. My hands held his cheeks as his lips pressed mine apart. Energy replaced the sadness I was feeling as his fingers lightly traveled to the back of my dress, locating my zipper and sliding it down.

"Yes," he whispered, and warmth flooded my stomach from both his words and the touch of his hands sliding across my back. "I'm not losing my angel."

My hands dropped to his untucked shirt, slipping to the skin beneath it. Our mouths reunited, and we were lost in preparing for the shortage ahead.

What was coming wasn't ideal, but we'd made it through worse than distance. The ties that had grown between us were stronger than ever, and should they waver, I only had to look down at my hand to know how he felt and what we had.

I remembered his explanation when he'd shown me his small tattoo. Dragonflies meant deeper understanding. They meant new beginnings, and in some cultures they meant good luck.

Standing here now, with him in my arms, I knew we had all three.

~ ~ ~

If you enjoyed this book by this author, please consider leaving a review at Amazon, Barnes & Noble, or Goodreads!

* * *

Be the first to know about New Releases by Leigh Talbert Moore! Sign up for the New Release Mailing list today at http://eepurl.com/tzVuP.

* * *

Mosaic, Book 4 in the Dragonfly series, coming 2014!

Mosaic
by Leigh Talbert Moore

The future never works out as expected.
People are not always how they seem.
And time changes everything.

The story that began in *Dragonfly*, grew more complex in *Undertow*, and culminated in *Watercolor* finds resolution in *Mosaic*.

For updates, follow Leigh Talbert Moore on Facebook, or sign up for her New Release Newsletter today!

Acknowledgments

First, I want to thank everyone who has read the Dragonfly series and loved it. This was my first big story idea, and it has meant so much to me that you've embraced it and loved it as much as I do.

So many readers have been excited for this third book, and your enthusiasm has kept me going through revisions and exhaustion. Thank you!

My faithful beta readers and cheerleaders in Baldwin County, Tracy Womack and Kim Barnes—I love you guys!

To my Facebook and Twitter friends—you guys are the best. I love your notes on teasers, ideas about taglines, enthusiasm about giveaways, enthusiasm about everything… You make my job so much fun.

To the book bloggers who love it—Ilaria, Anncleire, Gabby, Asheley, Roxy, and too many more to name—you guys are invaluable to me! Thank you so much.

And to my fantastic marketing crew, KP, Nazarea, and Nereyda. You are *invaluable* teammates.

To my lovely cover designer, Jolene Perry, and my awesome critique partners, Susan, Hart, Magan, and my best editor, my dear husband Richard. Thank you for keeping me going.

Finally, to my family and friends, who I love and miss. Thank you for being so patient, understanding, and supportive.

I couldn't do this without each and every one of you!

About the Author

Leigh Talbert Moore is a wife and mom by day, a writer by day, a reader by day, a former journalist, a former editor, a chocoholic, a caffeine addict, a lover of great love stories, a beach bum, and occasionally she sleeps.

Also by Leigh Talbert Moore:

The Truth About Faking (2012)
Rouge (2012)
The Truth About Letting Go (2013)

Dragonfly, Book 1 in the Dragonfly series (2013)
Undertow, Book 2 in the Dragonfly series (2013)

All of Leigh's books are available on Amazon, Barnes & Noble, iTunes, and Kobo.

Connect with Leigh online:

Blog: http://leightmoore.blogspot.com
Facebook: http://www.facebook.com/LeighTalbertMoore
Amazon Author page: amazon.com/author/leightmoore
Goodreads: http://www.goodreads.com/leightmoore
Twitter: https://twitter.com/leightmoore
Tumblr: http://leightmoore.tumblr.com

CPSIA information can be obtained at www.ICGtesting.com
Printed in the USA
BVOW01s1607190514

353957BV00005B/171/P